MOON
PEOPLE
3

MOON
PEOPLE
3

VENUS

THE GODDESS OF LOVE

"Best Sci-Fi In 2010"
"Amazon Gave Moon People 5 Stars"

Dale M. Courtney

To order additional copies of this book, contact:
Xlibris Corporation
1-888-795-4274
www.Xlibris.com
Orders@Xlibris.com
66874

TABLE
OF
CONTENTS

INTRODUCTION

T HANK YOU FOR reading my book Moon People 3. My goal in Moon People 3 was to make it as action pact from start to finish just like my first two Moon People books. I had to make a "Grand Finale" so I put everything into Moon People 3. I would also like to talk to you about the Venus genesis in this book for a moment. All of the Venus technical data is accurate and the Venus genesis formula is based on an actual analytical possible "Venus Genesis". It took me a while to figure out a true Venus genesis possibility. Because of the real high pressure in the atmosphere and on the surface. Also the very high temperatures on the surface. If It wasn't for me trying to figure out how to do a genesis on Mars and Venus. I would not have believed it possible. But now I believe it really can be done on both planets, Mars and Venus and maybe easier than we all thought. You know it is true that we can not go beyond our solar system because of distance and time in our life cycle. But I submit that we should be concentrating on the planets in our solar system. Could you imagine if we could pull off a Venus genesis or even a Mars genesis. We could colonize another planet in our solar system. Wouldn't that be the ultimate! Besides all of the above. I hope you don't mind but I just had to add some "Action Pack Sci-Fi Space Adventure" to the mix also. I hope you enjoy my book Moon People 3. I really enjoyed writing it for you. If you like Moon People 3, I hope you will read 1 And 2 also. I know you will enjoy them. If you have any questions or comments please e-mail me at:

Fishinghole1112000@yahoo.com
Thank you for your time and God Bless.
Author
Dale M. Courtney

VENUS GENESIS

Chapter 1

THIS STORY BEGINS in the year Oct. 6, 2050 orbiting the planet of Venus. Where Admiral Benson and the crew of the Aurora are in position. They are investigating if a Venus genesis is possible. Ever since 1st Science Officer Commander David Braymer successfully did a Mars genesis. All everybody has been saying is lets try Venus because its just like Earth and so close.

Mars is going great, its been a little over 1 year and yet construction on Mars because of light speed capability has advanced very rapidly. Their already at small city status and moving right along.

They now had a population of about 30,000 people. The Martians all survived thanks to Earth and the Powleens. Even 90 % of all of the animals on Mars survived. Earth brought animals, fish, trees, plant life, also a lot of plankton. Mars did not look anything like it use to. It looked like another Earth now. You could now see instead of a red planet you could see green and brown and blue all over its surface. It looked just like Earth except there was more land, a lot more land than water. But it was still a beautiful sight to see. Now everyone wants to do the same to Venus, if it is possible. The one that received most of the credit for the Mars genesis was Commander David Braymer 1st Science Officer on board the Lunar Base 1 mobile base station. He was famous on three planets, Earth, Mars and also Sybon. Sybon is the fourth planet from the star called An tares from the constellation of Scorpio where our friends the Powleens live. Mars was a thriving planet now. Construction was progressing all over Mars. Everyone was planting trees and bushes, plants of all kinds everywhere on Mars.

There was also construction material all over Mars too. New people arriving everyday from Earth and Sybon to colonize Mars. It was a fresh new planet coming to life again. Mars was literally resurrected from the dead. It was a beautiful time for Mars. There were Martians, Earthlings and Powleens living on Mars. There were even some captive Arcons and even some Thracians too.

There were even some of the Earthlings spreading the gospel to not just the Powleens but to Martians and Arcons and Thracians. I guess the idea was that they hoped that they took the knowledge back to their world. They also had another race called Koruins that the Arcons had enslaved from another world, century's ago. They had been abandoned by there own people because of war with the Arcon and the Thracian people. After the war we rounded up all of the Arcons and Thracians that crash landed on all of the planets and moons in our solar system that survived. Then we brought them all to Mars to study. We kept them all in a large luxurious apartment compound enclosed by the Martian shields. They were treated very descent. Some of them even felt bad for what they had done to everyone. They were living better on Mars than they had it on there own planets. Everyone new the Arcons and their friends couldn't have helped them at the time. Because they were high tailing it out of our solar system. Going back home with their tails between their legs as fast as they could. Earth was starting to learn a lot about our foe's the Arcons and the Thracians. It has been pretty peaceful since we won the war against the Arcons and the Thracians, the beginning of last year. We haven't heard a peep out of that sector of the galaxy since. We were also learning a lot about our new friends the Powleens. A very honorable race of people. In fact they were willing to die for their beliefs like us but were a peaceful race. To Earth, they were heaven sent. They had already saved Earth and all of the people twice. If it wasn't for them we wouldn't have light speed capability either. As David sat back with his hands locked behind his head. He was thinking, What if we could do the same thing on Venus? That would be so cool, we would have three planets that was inhabited with People. I have a feeling its not going to be as easy as Mars though. But I'm going to give it all I can to do it. I know at least it should be better than it was, I'm going to think positive about this. Who knows we might just get lucky on this one too, and if we do, that would be unbelievable! Then David started thinking about his girl friend Lieutenant Heather Courtney. Whom he met last year in the war to control the galaxy off of the planet Mars on board the Lunar Base 1.

David was becoming very much in love with her and was contemplating getting a lot more serious. But David wasn't ready for marriage. He couldn't quite get himself to go all the way but he knew if he ever did get married, she would probably be the one. We arrived at Venus two months earlier Aug. 5 and everyone has been studding the atmosphere. David found that there was several toxic chemicals in the air, mainly sulfuric acids and other sulfides. The entire atmosphere was mostly Carbon Dioxide, in fact it was right at 96.5 %. The rest was 3.5 % nitrogen and a few other things, Venus had the worse case of green house gas in the solar system. It was the hottest planet in the solar system too, because of that Carbon Dioxide. It was even hotter than Mercury which is closer to the Sun.

The atmospheric pressure on the surface was so high it was like being 1000 feet beneath the Earths ocean surface and it was also 465 degree Celsius at the surface of Venus at mid day. Its hellish surface has a boiling temperature that makes rocks glow red under a crushing atmosphere. The planets orbital speed is 35.02 km/3. The diameter of Venus was 6,051.9 km. Real close to Earth's size. Venus's atmospheric pressure at its surface was 92 times that of Earths surface. Now David was sure the problem was in the Carbon Dioxide. He knew that if he could fix the Carbon Dioxide problem and the temperature and pressure problem and get some Sun and water on the surface, he just might be able to pull it off. Also if he could increase the magnetic field of Venus it would be even better.

He also had to reduce the temperature way down to like 25 degrees Celsius. He had been studding the Carbon Dioxide problem for a couple of weeks. He knew the answer was in photosynthesis. So he started working out a solution. Now that the Aurora was fully staffed, David had a science department of over one hundred members. Everyone was concentrating on the Venus genesis.

On Earth the ionosphere is isolated from the solar wind "a flow of charged particles from the sun" by the magnetosphere, the magnetic envelope created by the dynamo effect of the Earths rotating core. Earth's magnetosphere deflects some Ion radiation and charged particles from the Sun. Although some particles can strike the atmosphere at the poles to create auroras.

Venus lacks a magnetic field of its own, but the solar wind seems to generate an induced magnetosphere around the planet by interacting with the ionosphere. This magnetosphere is similar to ones created around Comets. David just kept staring at the formula of photosynthesis. He just wouldn't stop going over the formula. The general equation for photosynthesis formula is : $CO_2 + 2 H_2A + Photons = (CH_2O)n + H_2O + 2A$ Carbon Dioxide + Electron Donor + Light Energy = Carbohydrate + Oxygen + Oxidized

Since water is used as the electron donor in oxygenate photosynthesis, the equation for this process is : $CO_2 + 2 H_2O + Photons = (CH_2O)n + H_2O + Sunlight =$ Carbon Dioxide + Water + Light Energy = Carbohydrate + Oxygen + Water.

David felt that the answer was the combination of water and CyanoBacteria and the Sun. He also was thinking if we release the combo in the upper atmosphere the photosynthesis would get more Sun. Maybe if we did both, release on the surface and the outer atmosphere it would be slow but steady. David also knew that the temperature on the surface was way to hot for any bacteria to survive.

The CyanoBacteria had to handle as much heat as possible. The temperature and pressure was two of the major problems in the experiment. The temperature might be repaired by creating a chemical reaction something like Freon when it gets exposed to heat in common air conditioning. The liquid evaporates and removes the heat, although Freon does put a lot more greenhouse like gases in the atmosphere, it also puts off a lot of poisonous gas when it burns. The world used this type of poison gas in World War 1 and 2 so we can't use Freon. There are other chemicals that will do the same thing as Freon but not burn or when it does burn, it does not put off poison gas. Nitrogen is one of the over all chemicals that most planets use as their air conditioning Freon.

Venus has 3.5 % nitrogen and Earth has about 78 % nitrogen in our atmosphere. What we can do to aid the chemicals on the surface is, we could make a ecliptic satellite adjustable tent shield. We could block the Sun out by eclipsing Venus. Surprisingly, on the night side of Venus, the upper atmosphere is extremely cold.(Day-side temperatures in the upper atmosphere are 40 degree C /104 Degrees F) compared to the (night temperature of -170 Degrees C/-274 Degrees F). David's Science department believe that strong winds blow from the day side toward the near vacuum that is caused by the low temperatures on the night side. Such winds would carry along light gases, such as Hydrogen and Helium, which are concentrated in a night-side "bulge". We only need to cool her as much as we can so we can do the photosynthesis experiment. David knew that when ever you have high temperature you will always have high pressure. David also knew, It's the same on the other end. When ever you have low temperature you will always have low pressure. We could implement everything and then take the shield away and let the Sun do its photosynthesis. He knew it just might work, but it would have to be done on a massive scale to do it. We might have to cool off Venus for a couple of days to see if it will work first. We now have ways to compress molecules very small so we can store a lot more volume, a 100 times more volume. For instance we can store enough chemicals in one canister to cool off 500 square mile radius.

We can change the chemistry on some types of gas easily to a harmless gas sometimes. We have just never done it on this big of a scale. So I figure we should do it something like this:

1) Eclipse the planet Venus with a special ecliptic satellite to cool off the planet and lower the atmosphere pressure. But it has to be a total eclipse. Then we could saturate the surface with the Nitrogen and more photosynthesis Cyano-Bacteria and water mixture.

2) Find a large ice cavity deep in the Venus crust if possible and hit it with the microwave beam in the right spot for Oxygen and water on the surface. Also to help cool off Venus, if we can find water.

3) Do the photosynthesis with some type of Cyano-bacteria with water on a slow but steady application in the outer atmosphere.

We will have to design several applicators for the outer atmosphere for more of the solar energy effect, because of the inner atmosphere is so thick and dense. David knew there were a lot of ways we could fail. But that's what science is all about. You take step by step, then do a experiment, analyze all of the data. Then start all over again from scratch until you get the job done. You just try not to make it worse than it already is. David had his science department design all of the photosynthesis satellite applicators for the outer atmosphere. Also the canister applicators for a chemical reaction on the planets surface. They had to with stand extreme heat until the chemicals are released. David knew that we could cool the planets surface by eclipsing it first. But then David started thinking so what if the chemical tanks melt from the extreme temperature and pressure. It would still release all of the chemicals. One thing for sure is, if I accomplished my genesis there will be a lot of sugar on Venus. Because that's what the end result is when you do the photosynthesis with Cyano-bacteria, you literally turn Carbon Dioxide into Oxygen and make sugar. Well then I believe the first step is to try to find some huge ice cavity. In fact for this idea to work we had better find a lot of ice some where. We should x-ray the planet and go from there. David was working hard at his science station on the bridge. The Admiral had not arrived at the bridge yet, but was due any time. David communiqués his assistant Lieutenant Robert Plant that was back at the main science office. Hello Commander Braymer, how are you doing today. The Commander answered, I'm doing good Lieutenant. The reason why I called you is I was wondering how far along you all are coming on the applicators for the photosynthesis and the chemical dispensers for the surface?

(Lieutenant Plant) Well sir, we have a lot to do but we think we have the perfect design on the photosynthesis applicators. It was Captain Dopar's design. He has been helping a lot on this project. We can adapt the satellites easily sir, but we are having a little trouble with the canisters for the chemical package. (Commander Braymer) You know Lieutenant I was thinking. The canisters really do not have to last that long. Only long enough to reach the surface of Venus. After we cool off Venus, when we eclipse her. It will make things a lot easier. Lieutenant Plant, I have something else I want you all to construct. Lieutenant I want you to supervise this too. I want you to use two ecliptic satellites. So we can totally eclipse the planet Venus. It has to be a total eclipse! So make sure you can't get any light on the ecliptic side. Ask if Captain Dopar can help you with it. I just want an extra satellite in between one eclipse to make sure no light gets through or incase one satellite fails. Then suddenly the Admiral walked into the bridge and walked over to David. Hello Commander, the Admiral said, how's everything looking today? Commander Braymer replied good sir, I was just going over everything with my assistant Lieutenant Plant. Lieutenant go ahead and do what we talked about and I'll get back with you later. Lieutenant Plant answered, yes sir. Then Commander Braymer said, Admiral I believe I might have a beginnings of a pretty good strategy for our genesis. Oh really the Admiral answered. What do you have going Commander? Then Commander Braymer said well sir here goes.

THE RIGHT STRATEGY

Chapter 2

THE PLANET VENUS is a lot like Earth was before the giant comet hit it and gave us our oceans sir. In fact Venus is also like our future too, because of global warming. Venus has a Carbon Dioxide or greenhouse effect problem going on here sir, that's the worst in our solar system. Sir the Venus atmosphere is 96.5 % Carbon Dioxide and 3.5 % Nitrogen. In another words is, this is Earth's future if we don't figure out how to stop global warming on our planet Earth sir. I believe that Earth and Venus were in the exact same condition until that comet hit Earth and gave us our oceans and cooled off our planet. Sir I also believe that the answer might just be in, believe it or not, is one little leaf. Then the Admiral said, oh really a leaf Commander. How's that? Commander Braymer replied. Well you see sir, one thing a leaf doe's do is what scientist call photosynthesis sir. Oh, I know what you're talking about now Commander the Admiral said. You're talking about how a plant breaths in Carbon Dioxide and gives off Oxygen, aren't you Commander? Then Commander Braymer said very good sir, but on a more complicated scale sir. You see their are a few ways to have photosynthesis. Not only can you get Oxygen from plants or leaves you can also get oxygen from Cyano-bacteria photosynthesis and plankton photosynthesis too. The plankton in all of our oceans on the Earth give off 70% of our oxygen.

But you have to have three things. One is sunshine another is Carbon Dioxide and most of all, you need a electron donor which in our case is water. Sir, here is my plan of attack. I believe I have it in the correct procedure now.

1) Eclipse the planet Venus with two big ecliptic satellites in the right spot so we can cool off the planet and its atmosphere. But it has to be a total eclipse. We can position the Aurora in between the sun and Venus. Also in between the satellite's and Venus.

2) Then we need to find a large ice cavity deep in the Venus crust. Then we hit it with the microwave beam like we did Mars for Oxygen and water on the surface. This will help with the photosynthesis and to bring down the Carbon Dioxide to the surface. That will help cool off Venus if we can find any ice. Then saturate the surface with the chemicals. Nitrogen and the photosynthesis Mixture.

3) Last but not least. Do the photosynthesis with some type of Cyano-Bacteria with water on a slow but steady spray application in the outer atmosphere.

We believe we have a good design for several satellite applicators for the outer atmosphere for more of the solar rays and the photosynthesis effect. Because the atmosphere is so thick and dense normally only 10% of the solar rays hit the surface of Venus. Admiral, if we want we can do a little experiment just by positioning the Aurora between the Sun and Venus just to see how much cooling of the surface we will do with the eclipse. We can also check the reaction to the Carbon Dioxide. It will give us an excellent preview on the rest of the experiment. Then Admiral Benson said, that sounds like a good idea Commander. We could go ahead and do that now. Lieutenant Parson lets put ourselves between Venus and the Sun to a point of a full eclipse. Lieutenant Parsons answered, yes sir. Just let me do some configurations. Commander Braymer my instruments are saying we need to go to the eclipse coordinates of 38.324N and 74.089W star mark 87563. Is that what your instruments are saying? Let's see, ah yes your right on the money Lieutenant, the Commander replied. Then Commander Braymer said one more detail Admiral, another problem we have is all of the sulfuric acid that's in the atmosphere. The cloud particles on Venus mostly consist of sulfuric acid particles. That's what makes it shine like it does. Earth's atmosphere also contains a very thin haze of sulfuric acid particles in the stratosphere. On Earth however, sulfuric acid does not build up because rain carries it down to react with surface materials. On Venus the acid evaporates at the cloud base, which lies about 50km (31mi) above the surface, and remains in the atmosphere. Variations in the sulfuric acid content of the atmosphere indicates a lot of volcanic activity on the planets surface. The fact that almost all of Venus's atmosphere is CO_2 is not as strange as it might seem. In fact, the crust of Earth contains almost as much CO_2 chemically bound in the form of limestone, a mineral that forms in the presence of water, about 3.5% of the Venusians atmosphere is Nitrogen gas (N_2). By contrast, 78% of Earth's atmosphere is nitrogen. The actual amount of Nitrogen molecules in the atmospheres of both planets is virtually the same, however. Water and water vapor are extremely rare on the surface of Venus because of her hellish temperatures. Although there are some very cold area's on Venus surprisingly most people do not realize that Venus's crust could be insulating huge ice cavity's with water below the surface. Also on the night side of Venus the upper atmosphere is extremely cold (Day-side temperatures are 40 degree C/104 degree F, compared to the night-side temperatures of -107 degree C/-274 degree F. Sir where there is cold there could be ice and maybe water. Actually we might be able to do some basic refrigeration with the extreme difference in temperature.

You see most chemicals at liquid state just keep absorbing heat until it evaporates at certain higher temperature into a gas and when that happens the gas gets rid of the heat and then turns back into a liquid when this gas is exposed to a certain cooler temperature it turns back into a liquid or ice. Most chemicals turn into a liquid at there own certain special temperature and starts absorbing the heat around the chemicals like Freon refrigeration in your air conditioning. Nitrogen is one of these chemicals that refrigerate planets. We are going to use Nitrogen in the experiment sir. But we would still have to do something with the Carbon Dioxide though. One thing for sure, what we learn from this Venus's genesis will help us out on Earth's global warming.

Then Admiral Benson said, very good Commander its sounds like you have a good plan. I hope we can find ice in Venus like we did Mars. Commander can we do the experiment without water? No sir David replied. Well maybe, but it would take a lot more time to study a different way. I already have some people on that already and they haven't really came up with any alternatives for the water or electron donor. I mean feasible to the Venus project. On Earth we do not have a water problem like Venus so we never tried a different electron donor.

Because water is one of the best electron donors there is, when it comes to photosynthesis. Water is the purist solvent known to man. Suddenly Lieutenant Parsons spoke out. Admiral I have finished with the arrangements and we can now proceed to the ecliptic location sir. Admiral Benson looks over to Lieutenant Parsons and smiles and say's. Very good Lieutenant lets proceed. Lieutenant Parsons replied, yes sir. Leaving orbit now sir. The Aurora started to move out of orbit and headed to the ecliptic site. As they were getting closer to the exact location you could see the eclipse beginning to happen on the view screen on Venus. Never before have we eclipse this particular angle on Venus, and it might be relevant to the over all temperature drop on the planet surface for the experiment. Then finally the Aurora was in position and there was a total eclipse on Venus. Then Commander Braymer said sir, our temperature probes on the planet surface are showing and instant decline in temperature. We are at 400 Degrees Celsius and falling sir, 350 Degree Celsius and still falling, 300 Degree Celsius and still falling sir.

CHILL OUT

Chapter 3

TEMPERATURE IS STARTING to fall more rapidly now sir. We are at 225 degree Celsius and still falling. Sir we are at 125 degrees Celsius and still falling, Sir the temperature fall is starting to slow. Admiral we are at -30 degrees Celsius and still falling, but really starting to slow and stabilize sir. Admiral we are stopping around -65 degrees Celsius. sir, we are starting to show liquid on the surface. (Admiral Benson) Commander my guess is that's liquid Nitrogen correct? David replied, unknown sir. Probably Nitrogen and a lot of frozen Carbon Dioxide too. Admiral I truly believe we might be able to do the genesis sir. The eclipse experiment worked better than anticipated Admiral. If we can find an ice cavity, we very well may be able to make another inhabitable world. Wow, I can't believe the words that came out of my mouth. That would be so fantastic. The Admiral looked over at David and said I agree Commander. Do you really think we might be able to do another genesis like Mars? Mars went from this:

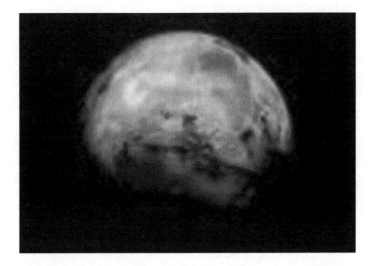

To Now this:

Commander Braymer answered maybe sir, if all of our data holds up. But we should be able to make it better than it was and then start all over again preferably in a lot better starting position. Or we might get lucky like Mars. We very well may be able to do it now sir. Then Admiral Benson said you have my vote Commander. So what do you want to do next Commander. Well Admiral I guess we could set up the ecliptic satellites why were here at location. Then go on the north west side of Venus and x-ray for ice cavities deep in her crust and prey its water. Or at least maybe have some water in the ice cavity. Then everyone noticed all of a sudden the atmosphere was clearing.

Lieutenant Courtney with communications said wow that's looking really clear. (Commander Braymer) Yes Lieutenant when the chemicals in the atmosphere started turning into a liquid. It fell to the surface like rain and absorbed the sulfur particles and other chemicals out of the outer atmosphere and took it to the surface too. Earth has almost the exact amount of sulfur oxides in its atmosphere but our rain brings it to the surface and mixes into are water ways and does other things. The sulfuric acid particles in the outer atmosphere is what makes Venus shine so bright and we removed it. Also sir, volcanic activity has almost slowed to a stop sir. Then Admiral Benson said, ok very good Commander. Lets proceed as you directed Commander. Let me know what's going on. I am going to my office for a little while to do a few things. Just let me know when you have set the satellites in place, ok Commander? David said, yes sir. Admiral I will keep you informed as we go sir. Then the Admiral said very good Commander and exited the bridge. Then Lieutenant Courtney interrupted and said Commander Braymer you have a communiqué from Bud Walker head of NASA. Very good Lieutenant patch him through to me. Hello Bud how's things on Earth going? Bud Walker answered, Pretty good Commander, we were just watching you and your Venus project. All of us down here on Earth are rooting for you no end. By the way Venus lost its shine. You can see it clear with all of Earths telescopes because its so close to the Earth but it's not even close to the brightness it use to be because its eclipsed.

How's it going way out there Commander? (David) Real good, the test we just did was very successful. My science department and I believe we can now do a genesis on Venus. We do need one more peace of luck and that is water. We need to find water and that's not going to be easy because Venus is such a hellish planet, so dry. But looks can be deceiving, because some planets crust is so thick and dense that it insolates the ice cavity's. Most planets have ice under their surface even though it may be a hot planet. Because of gravity when a comet hit's a planet the ice melts and puts Oxygen and water on the surface and then it goes to its lowest point that it can from centrifugal force. Then usually freezes. Then Bud said you said that well Commander. That's right you use to be a teacher. That would be great if you pulled this genesis off. The whole world would be astonished. When you have the time, would you send us your data so we can help in anyway possible? Everybody down here would love to help. The whole world's watching, so is Mars and Sybon on NASA's science T.V. station. We even get thousands of ideas on line from everywhere on how to do this and how to do that. We are even getting communiqués from Sybon wanting a progress report on Venus. Then David said that's great Bud. Sure we'll send you all of our up to date findings, and if anyone comes up with anything don't hesitate to give us a call. (Bud) Ok that's supper Commander we really do appreciate it, and if we come up with any ideas. We will give your science department a communiqué. (David) You got it Bud I'll catch you later sir. End the communiqué with NASA Lieutenant and send them down all our up to date data on the Venus genesis project. Also Lieutenant contact science engineering and get me a status report on the readiness of the ecliptic satellites and a possible time of launch. Lieutenant Courtney answered yes sir. I will get right on it sir. Now Lieutenant Charles Courtney the communications officer was one of the best there was in communications but he was also known to be kind of a prankster. He also loved to flirt with all of the women on board. The Lieutenant and a couple of his buddy's are all known as party goers. He has been trying to get a date with Lieutenant Parsons the pilot for a long time. But she seems to be on to him and turns him down all the time. But he doesn't stop flirting for fun. Lieutenant Jenna Parsons the pilot one of the best and her close friend Lieutenant Tawny Fisher the copilot do like Charles and they know he's a good guy and that he's only playing.

They were both in there mid 20s and two very attractive young lady's. They were also good friends with David's girl friend Lieutenant Heather Courtney, Lieutenant Charles Courtney the communication officer's sister. But one thing that stuck out on Lieutenant Charles Courtney was he had a reputation of being a playboy. Since they defeated sexual transmitted diseases back in 2030 and the sexual revelation of 2034. Sex has been pretty much open for adults. It was a way of cementing a very close friendship and there was also a element of play connected to sex now. With more open partners than ever before. Ever since they abolished marital alimony except for bad health, and equal custody for the children in a divorce. The divorce rate went way down but so did the marriage rate. Then Lieutenant Charles Courtney spoke up, Commander I just got off the phone with science engineering sir. They are ready to launch the two ecliptic satellites for the experiment. Commander Braymer replied very good Lieutenant. Tell them to go ahead and launch the satellites in position. As soon as they are in position we will go x-ray Venus at these coordinates Lieutenant Fisher, lat.45Nw27.99 and long. 30Ne45.12. Lieutenant Fisher sounded out, roger that Commander. Commander Braymer they are launching the satellites now sir. They should be in location in about 7 minutes Commander. (David) Very good Lieutenant Parsons, thank you. Then Commander Braymer hit his communicator button on his coat and said Computer contact Lieutenant Heather Courtney! (Computer) Affirmative. (Heather Courtney) Hello David how's it going. (David) Hey honey, pretty good how's everything where your at? OK Heather replied, I'm just down here at the main laundry room trying to find my best blue dress. It wasn't in the laundry shoot this time either, it should have came back through the air shoot in the last three bundles and that's my best dress. I am not going to loose that dress. By the way David do you know what tomorrow is? David answered, No what? Don't you remember silly, Heather asked? Its our 1 year anniversary. David said Oh yeah, your right. We're going to have to celebrate. What do you want to do tomorrow to celebrate? Well Heather answered, I don't know. Do you want to go out at a restaurant or do you want to eat at your place and maybe watch a movie like we did when we first met? David smiled and said, Hmm. I don't know honey they both sound good to me. I'll do either one. Then Heather said, what do you say we do both. We can go out to eat at Oceans Red Lobster and see that new fish aquarium they just installed. It takes up the whole wall they say. Then we can go to your place and watch a movie and have some wine. Suddenly Lieutenant Courtney said Commander, engineering has just confirmed that the two satellites are now in place sir. Then David said, can you hold a minute honey? Heather replied, sure baby, go ahead. Then David answered, very good Lieutenant. Lieutenant Parsons lets head on over to our coordinates and maybe we can get a couple of x-rays, and just see what's over there. God I hope there's water over there. Also contact Admiral Benson and brief him on everything. (Lieutenant Parsons) Commander we are moving out of position now sir and heading to your location. David answered, very good Lieutenant. Oh I'm sorry honey. Lets see why don't we do both. I can sure dig some sea food, that would be great. I heard that the fish aquarium was finished too and that it looked great. OK, you have your self a date then sweetheart. I hope you find your dress. I know what dress your taking about and I think you look great in that dress too. Heather smiled and said thanks David, If I find my dress I will wear it tomorrow when we go out. OK honey David replied, I'm going to go ahead and let you go, I love yeah baby. (Heather) I love you to David. Then David said Computer end communiqué. As David was watching the Aurora moving in place, it was a beautiful sight to see on the main viewer. You could see the surface from space much clearer now. Before the atmosphere was to dense. Now the Pressure and Temperature is way down to almost bearable levels. Lieutenant Parsons spoke out. Commander we are now at our coordinates. Ok Lieutenant let me do some figuring and here goes. We will take two x-rays here and then we will move over to that icy valley over their, David pointed at a certain location on the view screen. Lets take two x-rays over there and then my staff will analyze our findings. So will our computer to see what we have. David did a couple calculations and then took two x-rays and said, ok Lieutenant I just completed the x-rays here. Lets go over to that big valley to the north and we will take two more there. Computer analyze the x-ray's that we just took for ice cavity's in the planets crust and show me the data. Affirmative, working. Then all of a sudden it came up on David's monitor. There was all kind of ice below the surface but we didn't know if it was water or something else. Bingo, we have all kinds of ice signs. Then, in walked the Admiral and he told everyone hello and told David he had been watching in his office. So he came right down when he seen how far a long he was. Then Commander Braymer said, Admiral perfect timing, guess what we just found? The Admiral asked did you find water? Not sure yet sir, David answered. We did how ever find all kinds of Ice cavity sign though. (Admiral) Very Good Commander. What's our next step? Well sir David replied, we are going to take two more x-rays in that valley over there and again he points to the view screen. Then I guess its up to you if you want to try the microwave beam then sir. Then the Admiral said, I can see you are moving right a long here Commander. I just hope it works or at least better than it was. NASA reported that Venus lost its shine and I know its because of the eclipse, but I just don't want it to be worse after we are done, I guess. Lets just hope we pull it off, that would be so cool. Lieutenant Parsons interrupted. Admiral we are in position for the other two x-rays sir. David said affirmative Lieutenant. Let me take two more x-rays. It will only take a couple of seconds sir. There we go, I'm finished Lieutenant. Let me send these x-rays to my staff and then I will have the computer analyze what we have and make a couple of calculations. I will consult with my staff so we can determine where the right location is to hit the ice cavities with the microwave beam. All of this should take about 1 hour sir. I was also going to grab some lunch. Admiral replied very good, keep me informed Commander. David answered, yes sir.

David got up and left the bridge and went to his quarters. As he arrived at his quarters he ordered his lunch and with in 2 minutes it was at his kitchen and he was sitting down at his living room sofa watching his view monitor while he was eating his lunch. Then he hit his communicator button on his uniform and said computer connect me to Captain Freedman or Lieutenant Plant in the science department office. This is Captain Freedman, hello Commander how's things on the bridge? David answered, oh pretty good. I'm not on the bridge though. What I need you to do is get all of your project heads together. We need to do more planning on the procedure on where to hit the ice cavity's with the microwave beam. So we can get this right in about an hour ok. I will tell you what I came up with and then you can tell me what you guy's came up with and we will go from there. (Captain Freedman) Yes sir, I will get right on it. Then David said, one more thing Captain I'll need your report in a hour. All I'm looking for right now is proper location to hit the ice with the microwave beam. We might as well start on the rest of the genesis project from this point on. Like do we do the microwave beam now or wait for more time for the planet to cool from the eclipse? I believe that we would be better off if we did the microwave beam with the eclipse on. So our next step might be implementing the microwave beam now. Then we can see if there is water in the ice cavity and if we get Oxygen in the atmosphere or not. But right now we should find the right location to hit the ice cavity with the microwave beam. I believe we should hit the cavity dead center like we did Mars. Captain Freedman replied very good sir, I will get right on it. Then David said, thank you Captain. Computer end communiqué. This steak and shrimp lunch is really good. Lets see first, we should hit the ice cavity with the beam. Then check and see if there's water and Oxygen. Then we can plant the canisters of nitrogen and the photosynthesis mixture on the surface of Venus.

THE GODDESS OF LOVE

Chapter 4

THEN ALL WE have to do is spray the water and bacteria mix from the applicators in the outer atmosphere. Then take away the eclipse or tone it down a bit and watch it work. Boy I hope this works as easy as it sounds? This reminds me of a old Earth commercial for shack and bake, and the phrase was Shack and Bake and I helped. Then suddenly David's door bell sounded off and when he opened the door he seen a pretty sight. It was Heather and she figured he would be here at this time. Because he is usually here at or around this time of day for lunch when there isn't anything going on. David was stunned Heather was so beautiful looking. Well hello honey, I was just thinking about you. Then David took a more intent look, and said you look as pretty as Venus the Goddess of love her self. Then Heather gave David a very sexy look and with a sexy manor she leaned in and said thank you David. I thought I would stop by and see if you were here for lunch. Then Heather gave David another sexy smile and said I thought I might get lucky. Then David started snickering and said no it looks like I'm the one that might get lucky. Then David leaned in and started kissing Heather and said you know honey there is nothing in the whole wide world I would rather do than to make love to you. But unfortunately for me, I can not right now because we have this Venus genesis going down. I have to leave in a few minutes to go to my science office for a couple of minutes and then back to the bridge. But I do appreciate the thought though. In fact if you want to come back about 0500 I would love to start back up where we left off. Then Heather replied oh you would, would you. Well I don't know, I don't get turned down much. Heather gave a funny look and said, In fact I don't think that I have ever been turned down before. I will see what I can do though. Then David said did you ever find your blue dress? Heather answered, no I didn't, but they said it would show up eventually. So I'll just have to wait. Then David said, it will show up, you'll see. David smiled again and said where's it going to go.

Unless we jettisoned it in outer space, it's got to be here somewhere. I'm the Commander and I never heard the order to jettison your dress, David smiled again. All right now, you win, Heather said. I'm going to go for now but you just might see me around 0500 though.

Then Heather gave David a long and erotic kiss and said your my genesis man and chuckled. Then David said you know honey now I can't wait for 0500 for some reason. They kissed one more time and then Heather left and David took off for his science department. As David arrived at his office, he quickly unloaded from the air shuttle and went in the office. Everyone was in the conference room going over all of the details of the photosynthesis project from start to finish. Then David walked in the conference room and said good afternoon everyone. I thought I would come down and join you here for the final layout of the project. Well Captain Freedman what did all of you come up with? Then Captain Freedman replied, sir we have went over everything several times and this is the procedure that we came up with.

1) Well sir, the first thing we thought might be the microwave beam on the ice cavity. Hoping that we find water.
2) Second, place the Nitrogen canisters on the surface. Each canister holds enough Nitrogen for a 500 mile radius.
3) Then we launch all of the photosynthesis applicators in the outer atmosphere around Venus.

Then sir all we have to do is get out of the way of the sun. Then David spoke up and said that's exactly what I came up with too Captain. Very good everyone. Let me show all of you this on the view screen David said. There we go. Here is where I was wanting to hit the ice cavity. That is the center of the cavity. Everyone looked at where David was pointing on the screen and they were all in agreement. Everybody you've done a great job here on this Venus genesis. We still have a whole lot to do, so I just want all of you to know that this may not do the trick, but it should get us closer to our goals. There's only one way to find out our answers. I'm going to go back to the bridge and get started on everything. But don't worry everyone will get credit for this project. I will make sure of that. Ok, now I guess we can get going on all of the canister applicators and the satellite applicators. Oh, well I had better get back to the bridge. Once again good job everyone. Then David left and went back to the bridge. When he arrived, Admiral Benson was on the bridge going over protocol with everyone.

Hello Commander is everything still looking good. Yes sir David answered, I just left my office where we had a big conference on the genesis. We are all unanimous sir, on procedure. I recommend we hit the ice cavity dead center like we did Mars. Then place the canisters on the surface. Then we launch the satellite photosynthesis applicators.

Finally sir, we can get out of the way of the sun sir or tone it down a hair! Outstanding Commander the Admiral replied, it sounds like we have a good plan. Well Commander what do you say you get situated at your station and we get started on the genesis project. David answered Very good sir. David sat down at his station and started turning on all of his monitors and equipment. Then when he was ready he said, sir I'm all ready now and if you like, I can ready our microwave beam. We just need to warm it up a couple of minutes. Admiral if you want, Lieutenant Parsons can fire the beam on your mark. I thought we would do it like we did on Mars. You know sir, fire the beam at 3 second intervals starting out. Then increase if needed sir. Then the Admiral said, very good Commander. If your ready Lieutenant we will fire the microwave beam. Lieutenant Parsons smiled at the Admiral and then said, I'm ready for your mark sir. Excellent Lieutenant, the Admiral replied, go ahead and fire on my mark Lieutenant. (Lieutenant Jenna Parsons the pilot) We are all go here sir. Then the Admiral said ok Lieutenant fire the microwave beam on full power for three seconds! Yes sir, the Lieutenant replied, firing now sir. From space you could see a yellow beam that was encircled around a middle yellow beam. The microwave beam had 200,000 watts of power coming out of the ship and by the time it hit's the surface it's about 50,000 watts and by the time it gets to the ice cavity beneath the surface it is about 20,000 watts of power and was also a very effective weapon if needed. It seemed to penetrate through every-ones shields except the Martian ships in the war last year. The microwave beam lost a lot of its power when it did penetrate their shields but it was still able to penetrate enough power to start a low frequency microwave heating effect to cause a lot of damage. But we would rather use it in a genesis project, like this one or the Mars genesis. With the help from the Martians we are putting all of the Martian shields and weapons on all of earth's space-fleet. The Powleens are also doing the same thing to their space-fleet too. The Martian weaponry advanced the Powleens to be the most powerful world in the galaxy because of their size, They already had the biggest and the most powerful space fleet in our galaxy but their weaponry was like ours. Now all three planets have the Martian weapons. We don't mind the Powleens having the weapons because they already had power over the galaxy and they treated everyone with kindness and generosity. If it wasn't for the Powleens we would have never had gotten light speed and many other future technology's. They also saved Earth twice and Mars in the war for control of the galaxy.

We do a lot of trade with the Powleens and they have always treated us with fairness and kindness. They helped out a lot with the Mars genesis too, and ask nothing in return except for fair trade. Another big event is the President and the Powleens have made another large trade deal for twenty more of their ships of all kinds to us. They all had light speed capability. It seems that Earth has a lot of minerals and food and plants and trees and fish that the Powleens like. Earth has a lot more trees and vegetables and life forms than the Powleens home planet. Plus the fact that the Powleens really do like us. The way they see us is that they have only had good luck with us and they really admire us for doing these genesis's. I guess it is that Mars was so successful. If the Arcons and the Thracians ever came back they will be defenseless with the weapons we have now. Because of the Martians we became very powerful with their shields and fire power. Their weapons now can't even penetrate our shields. We seen in the war last year that everything the Martians had was so far ahead of everyone else. The Arcons didn't have a chance. The

Aurora has already fully completed with the installation of the Martian shields on board and they were working on the Martian weapons at present but they are not working at this time. We are going to have one of the Martians for a science officer soon to assist Commander Braymer. Commander Braymer really wanted the Martians in his science organization. They would be a big asset on board our ship as we go all over the universe.

They are way advanced to even the Powleens. The Powleens even wanted some Martians on their planet because they were so advanced. Everyone was getting along so well on Mars. Mars was a major success. Even some of the Arcon prisoners liked it on Mars. We were learning a lot about the Arcons and Thracians prisoners and how they lived and their diet. They had a ferocious appetite. We were also learning a lot more about the Martians and all of their mental powers too. They even loved our television shows and our movies. They were just like us. They could easily access our satellites on Earth for our television networks and communication networks and their translators would translate the movies easily for them. On Mars you could see them watching all of the shows on Earth and laughing hard. The Martians and the Powleens both loved our video games the most. They were an incredible race. They could even fly by mental levitation for a short distance of about 1 mile but it would take all of their energy out of them. Dr. Moon on board the Aurora told the Martians not to levitate for a least six months, so they could gain their strength back. Kind of like a stop smoking kind of thing. When we were reviving the Martians after the genesis one of the nurses just touched one of the Martians and she immediately past out drained of all energy. She was all right though. Then the Martians figured out we were saving them and they loved us after that. They were so happy just to get a second chance of living in the solar system. We resurrected a little over 1200 Martian lives on the Mars genesis. That does not include all of their original native animals. There were over 700 Martians animals that survived.

We even saved some plants that they had in their lab. Of coarse we brought over a lot of Earths animals and people and a lot of plants and trees, flowers, Plankton and so did the Powleens. Mars had the best of all the planets. Mars was such a beautiful world now and the Martians couldn't be happier. They even said to themselves they weren't this happy when they were alive a 100,000 years ago. But they missed all of their friends and family that died from the meteor shower that wiped out their planet.

They were still very sad about that. They wrote all about their friends in books, and wrote a lot of story's about their past, they missed all of there people so much. The Martians were the leading alien world of the galaxy in their time. But they knew that what we had done was change their fate. So they were so happy to get a second chance in the solar system. They literally loved us, in fact they were so grateful, we knew that they would do anything we would ask. But we never ask them to do anything for what we did for them, except be our friends. We also found out something that was fascinating to know. We found out from Venal the ruler of Mars and his scientist's that the comet that hit Earth was our Moon. When it hit the Earth the impact was so great that it first melted the comet. Then it bounced off of the Earth in its present position and became our Moon and left all of its water on Earth that made our oceans. Kind of like if you had a truck full of water and it hit another car in a accident. Then the truck would bounce off of the other vehicle and leave it covered with water.

We reenacted the scenario in space in a weightless environment experiment. It did the exact same thing. The comet came from the constellation of Capricorn where one of it's stars went supper nova and shot it out into the galaxy toward us. Also the comet that hit us was once an inhabited planet like Earth. One of the Martian scientist named Barco also said that we might check our Moon for an ice cavity beneath its surface like you did us. The Powleens also traded twenty of their ships to the Martians in exchange for their shields and weaponry. We had already given the weapons and shields to the Powleens. They were so grateful though that they gave the ships to the Martians and Venal immediately ordered the installation of all of their weapons and shields and also they were adapting the Powleen Moon ship engines with their own engines to be put on board all of their Moon ships. Their engines were capable or light speed for very short distances, They would just appear and disappear without a sound barrier being broken, as quiet as a mouse. Their fighter crafts were very easy to fly and really neat to watch when they did disappear and reappear. We were going to wait for them to design the engines and then we were going to see if they would trade it to us for our fleet. He also put a lot of their Martian fighter crafts onboard their Moon ships. They were a real asset to the Martian Moon ships. Their may not be a lot of Martians on their planet but they have a very affective space fleet now. (Commander Braymer) Admiral I am showing no change on all of my instruments. I recommend doing a ten second interval this time. Admiral Benson answered, very good Commander. Lieutenant Parsons lets do it again except this time we will do a ten second interval. Lieutenant Parsons replied, yes sir.

Initiating now sir. A time counter came on the huge main view screen. 10, 9, 8, 7, 6, 5, 4, 3, 2, 1, you could also see the microwave ray hitting the surface of the planet. Sir the ten second interval is now finished. Then everyone seen steam shooting out all over on the surface of Venus like it did on Mars. Then David was analyzing the data from all of the probes that they had already put on the surface of Venus.

VENUS SHOWS SIGNS OF LIFE

Chapter 5

BINGO SIR, DAVID spoke out loud, we have Oxygen, among other things but we have Oxygen. Everyone shouted all right. Sir I'm still showing a lot more ice down below and another huge ice cavity back at the other coordinates we just left sir. Sir, I suggest we hit everyone of these ice cavity's and put all the Oxygen and water we can on the surface while we have the planet eclipsed. Also Admiral I believe we are cooling off the planet some just by eclipsing it for so long, not by what you see now. What I mean is when we go to take away the eclipse, the over all planet should be cooler than it was just from being eclipsed for all of this time. I agree Commander, the Admiral replied. Do you want to go three ten second intervals or just one more ten seconds only. (David) Admiral lets try 3 ten second intervals one time just to see if it is better to go a little harder instead of slow and steady. Then the Admiral said, ok Commander, Lieutenant lets accommodate the Commander and initialize the microwave beam for three, ten second intervals. Yes sir said Lieutenant

Parsons. First ten seconds beginning now sir, first 10 seconds complete. Second 10 seconds complete. Third 10 seconds is completed now sir. You could see the massive microwave beam turn on and off on the main view screen. It was a sight to see. Then suddenly Venus started spewing steam all over the north west side of the planet.

(Commander Braymer) Sir the experiment is working we are showing a lot more Oxygen on the surface. All of the sudden you could see Venus snowing at there location. It was coming down heavy, it was starting to accumulate on the surface. Before you knew it everything was clouding up. You could even start to see a upper jet stream starting to grow. Or a massive cold front forming. Everything was steaming up into the higher atmosphere and turning into snow. Then David said sir, I believe we are about out of ice at this location. Request we move to our last location where we found another huge ice cavity below the surface. Admiral Benson and everyone else was watching all of the snow on the view screen, it was a spectacular sight to see.

Then the Admiral said, Commander when you cook, you sure can cook, request granted Commander. Lieutenant Parsons take us to your last location. (Lieutenant Parsons) Affirmative sir. Going back to our last location now sir. The Aurora very gracefully moved from one location back to the other. Ok Admiral said David. I just need a couple of minutes to coordinate the right location to concentrate the microwave beam. Sir we have a huge ice cavity here. I would say about twice as big as the one we just left. If this is mostly water we should be in better shape Oxygen and water wise than Mars or as good.

One more thing Admiral, we could leave in place two or three satellites with just a slight tent to their ecliptic shield to them. So that just the right amount of Sun gets through. We can adjust it from the temperature on the surface. The reason I am saying this is just in case the Sun might be two hot and that we might have to tone it down a bit sir two maintain life or a colony. It all depends on the end result of this experiment though. David had a anxious look on is face and said, ok one more calculation and WA LA. Admiral I believe we have our correct coordinates laid in and we can fire one ten second interval just to warm up the area if everyone is ready. The Admiral answered, you got it Commander. Lieutenant what do you say we do it one more time?

Lieutenant Parsons gave the Admiral a big smile and said, affirmative sir. Here goes, suddenly you could watch the LED display on the large view monitor, count down from ten to zero. Then just like before you could see steam shoot out high into the upper atmosphere. As it cooled, it would turn into a big cold front and start dumping large amounts of snow back down all over the surface of Venus. Well Commander I like your work sir said the Admiral. Thank you sir but it is, all of us here taking the same amount of risk's and putting in the same amount of dedication. Well sir what do you say to trying three ten second intervals once on this ice cavity? I'm go if you are Commander, said the Admiral. OK Lieutenant lets do it one more time, lets do three, ten second intervals, the Admiral said. Lieutenant Parsons smiled and said I know sir, here we go again. Initiating the microwave now sir. Then suddenly on the main viewer you could see the microwave beam from the ship to the surface of Venus. It was quite a sight to see, a pretty yellow beam that wrapped around one single yellow beam all the way to the surface. On an off it went three times and finally it was done. Then without warning the top half of a volcano blew off into a thousand different pieces into the outer atmosphere. You could see steam shooting out all over the top half of Venus. Most of Venus's northern hemisphere was clouding over and then turning into massive snow storms but slow moving. Then everyone looked at David kind of funny. David started smiling back and said you know this is really not all that out of the ordinary. You see most volcano's seal themselves when they cool. The steam just built up until the volcano's top blew off. Then the Admiral starting laughing and said you have my vote Commander. Well what's next Commander the Admiral asked? Well sir I believe we should do it until we get as much Oxygen and water on the surface as we can for the experiment. I believe we should be alright now sir. We already blew the hole open for the rest to come out. Then the Admiral looked at David and smiled and said ok Commander what your saying about getting all of the water and Oxygen on the surface makes since to me. I'm going to go ahead and give the ok but if there are any more blow outs maybe we could rethink our strategies. Commander Braymer laughed and said you got it sir, but I really don't think we are going to see any more massive explosions sir. But it's not all that out of the ordinary with what we are doing. It could happen though. We really do not have much ice left sir about a third of what we started with. We might have about one more time with the three, ten second intervals that will probably do the trick sir. Then the Admiral said very good Commander. I just want you to know, I'm behind you 100%. The Admiral smiled and said ok Lieutenant, lets do three more 10 second intervals. Then Lieutenant Parsons said very good sir. Initiating first sequence. First sequence starting now sir. Then once again you could see the number count down come on the view screen. While the beautiful yellow beam turned on and off for yet three more time. The microwave beam was an incredible invention. How ever wide the diameter of the beam was, the interior of the beam was like a microwave oven. Kind of like a pre-laser kind of set up. It could also reach a high power of 200,000 watts. It was an amazing tool for these ice cavities deep in the planets surface. The entire surface was now clouding up, but our probes down on the surface was reporting massive amounts of snow accumulation and Oxygen. David's instruments were also showing large amounts of Oxygen and water. You could even now see a jet stream developing. The experiment was working good so far, better than expected. Even the Powleens were impressed by the microwave beam. It seemed that the surface was not taking long for the clarity of the atmosphere to clear up.

Venus was clearing fast and you could see the surface. It looked like Earth in the middle of winter.

One of our crew members that is a Powleen, that everyone on the bridge works with all of the time, was Captain Dopar, he was really impressed. He was as fascinated as much as we were. He more or less helped David on the bridge but was very active in the Aurora science department. We had technology that they didn't have and they had a lot of technology we didn't have like light speed capability, for one thing.

The Powleens liked us I believe because we were a lot like them. Also because we had a lot of neat inventions too. From our blenders to are computer extras. The Powleens also loved our mashed potato's and our banana's. The potato's and the banana's grew well on their planet. We still had about 50 Powleens on board. They were a tremendous asset to the crew of the Aurora. Everyone was starting to get optimistic about the genesis. Then Admiral Benson said, well Commander its looking really good.

I see what you were talking about earlier about possibly leaving one of the satellites in place with a slight tint to it to keep the planet at a certain temperature. Let me say, you people down in the science department are incredible with some of the stuff you come up with. Ok Commander where are we at now? Commander Braymer answered. Well sir, I guess we are just about done with this ice cavities. I thought there was more ice by volume than there was. It might have been something else like liquid Nitrogen that was frozen or among a thousand other chemicals. We are now showing that we have enough water and oxygen on the planet. I think we are in great shape for the genesis experiment sir. Sir to answer your question. I believe we are at the point of placing the Nitrogen canisters on the surface. I have been thinking too sir. We should go ahead and put the photosynthesis canisters on the surface too with the Nitrogen canisters sir. We will lower the tent on the satellites a little bit at a time. Then the Admiral said, you can do that Commander? (David) Yes sir we can turn down the tent, kind of like we turn down and up on the brightness knob on our television monitor. It was Captain Dopar sir. David's Powleen associate that developed the technical modification we needed to make it work. David was becoming very good friends with Captain Dopar. He still wasn't use to his size though the Captain was 7' 9" or 93" tall.

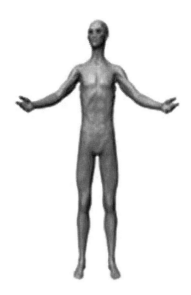

He had a little muscle base to him but his arms and legs and torso and neck were all elongated. His arm length was 72" long. But they were just like us in a lot of other ways. They even had a great sense of humor and they liked to party like us too. They were the same as us. Admiral I'm going to go ahead and start setting everything up sir.

It will probably take the rest of the day and most of tomorrow so I guess we will continue by setting all of the canisters on the surface by tomorrow and try to get all of the satellite applicators launched afterwards sir. Then the Admiral laughed and said, ok Commander I guess the excitement is over for most of the day then. What do you say we finish up everything we have going on the bridge. I will go to my office and get a few things done there for about two hours. Commander why don't you contact me when you are ready to do something else or just up date me on the genesis. I am proud to be in with you Commander, and congratulations on the genesis so far. "Well Done Commander". If you look at Venus now, it looks better than it was. You can tell we are not far off from finishing this genesis. I'm going to head to my office and check up on some details. I will see you maybe later on today or around 0600 tomorrow. David replied thank you sir, I will contact you later on today if we can do anything later. If we can't I guess I will see you tomorrow at 0600 then sir. Then the Admiral said very good Commander and proceeded to his office. On the way out the door he told Commander Craft that the helm was his. That left Commander Craft in charge of the bridge. Then David communiqués his science department and told them that he wanted to finish putting the photosynthesis canisters on the surface also with the Nitrogen canisters and they agreed. Then Captain Freedman and his group of science engineers started launching all of the canisters. They knew they could not finish today, they had a group from maintenance helping. There was also some cargo bay boys helping. Everyone started to get all of the canisters ready for launch to the surface of Venus. They were also preparing 78 satellite applicators for launch. Everybody worked hard for a good five hours, they weren't done but they called it a day.

Then everybody was to meet at the Red Star lounge for some drinks and to talk about their day. That was the normal routine after work most days or everyone would play cards or just clown around.

Head of Communications Lieutenant Charles Courtney everyone called chuck was well known at this lounge. He was known for his silver tongue, for he was a smooth operator with the lady's. He wasn't a bad guy though. He was very good at the game of chess too. Everyone also knew that he was famous for his practical jokes he pulled on people. There were a few people who wanted to get him back for the practical jokes he pulled on them so much so that there were innocent people getting caught in the middle from time to time. Lieutenant Courtney's sister, Commander Braymer's girl friend Heather, always kept David informed on all of the practical jokes stuff. Chuck used to pull a lot of jokes on Heather when she was young. So now she secretly plots against him for fun from time to time. When she finds out what joke he's trying to pull on somebody else. She try's to make them backfire on him, and he doesn't know it. Usually everybody arrives about 20:00 hours and today was no different in came Lieutenant Chuck Courtney and his two friends Specialist Mike Parker and his younger brother Corporal Steven Parker. They headed straight for the bar. They got their regular drinks and then went to their normal table.

(Corporal Parker) Hey Lieutenant did you ever get a date with Lieutenant Parsons? No I wish, Chuck replied, she is such a fox. I almost had a date with her up in the observatory on the Lunar Base 1 last year but the war happened and we never did.

I haven't been really trying all that hard lately. I think the reason why she don't go out with me is my sister. Well I'm not sure but I think my sister might be working against me on this one. I think she keeps saying all I want is to get into Gina pants and that's not true. I just wanted to go out with her.

The problem is I don't think anyone believes me. I admit I use to do a lot of practical jokes on people, but I don't now. I've learned my lesson a long time ago. Suddenly more people started walking in. This time it was some of the crew from the science department. Captain Freedman and Lieutenant Plant and two of their engineers. They had just finished with the canisters for the day, there were still more, they were just going to finish the rest of the canisters tomorrow morning.

They had a pretty good system. They were using man less probes that would deliver the canisters and then return to the Aurora on it's own. They were robotic and could function totally independent by voice command from the ship. They could withstand very high pressures and very hot temperatures up to 1500 degrees Fahrenheit and also very cold temperatures 300 below zero.

You could hear Captain Freedman talking about the canisters and also planning tomorrows launch of all of the photosynthesis satellite applicators. They worked pretty hard today they launched 196 canisters in the probes to the surface and back. Tomorrow they have a few canisters left and 78 photosynthesis satellite applicators to launch into the upper atmosphere. They are just basic satellites with the canister applicators on them. They will orbit in the outer atmosphere with periodic spraying of the photosynthesis mixer. Although some of the planets gases and charged particles has settled to the surface, absorbed from the snow fall. There are still chemicals in the outer atmosphere. The pressure now on the surface and in the atmosphere has reduced to expectable levels. When you have low temperature you will always have low pressure, they always go together. David thought the experiment will work better if the atmosphere was like sandwiched in between both applications of the photosynthesis experiment. Some how David just knew he was right. David didn't usually hang out at the Red Star lounge but he came there every now and then usually to meet Heather. Then he only drank a couple of drinks and they would either go to Heather's place or David's place. All of a sudden in walked Lieutenant Heather Courtney and her two Lieutenant friends

Jenna Parsons and Tawny Fisher. Lieutenant Jenna Parsons and Lieutenant Tawny Fisher was Admiral Bensons Pilot and Copilot from the beginning, all the way back to the Lunar Base 1. They graduated highest in there field and were the pilot and copilot on the Lunar Base 1 when it first launched it's maiden voyage to Mars from Earth. They were talking about the Venus genesis until they seen Chuck Courtney and his friends. Then they walked over to their table and said hi to everyone they also said hi to the Powleens over in the corner, Jenna and Tawny sat down for a minute. Heather walked over to the bar and ordered two beers one for her and one for David when he finally gets There. David agreed to meet Heather there for a couple of beers earlier.

Then just like clock work in walked David. He seen Heather right away and walked right over at the bar to her. Everyone at Chucks table said hello to Commander Braymer. David waved and said hey how's everything going everyone? Chuck said back, oh we should be ok here with a couple of beers sir. Then the Commander said I wouldn't over drink, you know how bad everyone gets the bed spins up here. Chuck replied I wont sir. That doesn't really affect me like it does everyone else sir.

Then David said it's just that we have a big day tomorrow Lieutenant. Lieutenant Chuck Courtney replied, you got it sir.

Commander do you think we might be able to pull off the genesis tomorrow like we did on Mars sir? David answered, God I hope so Lieutenant, wouldn't that be phenomenal? Then Chuck replied, yes sir. We sure would change things in our solar system for a very long time, wouldn't we sir. One thing for sure sir, tomorrow will tell it all.

(David) You got that right Lieutenant. If we pull off tomorrow we will make history, I hate to leave good company Lieutenant but I'm going to go back over to that beautiful woman at the bar. You guys and gals have a good day. Then everyone said you to sir and Commander Braymer walked back to Heather and gave her a big kiss and said, well how did your day go honey? Heather replied oh ok David. It would have been better if they would have found my blue dress though. You mean they still haven't found your blue dress yet David asked? Heather answered No, with a frustrated look on her face, David I fear it's gone for good. Then David said, oh honey it's got to be on this ship somewhere. It will show up. Where's it going to go? Heather smiled and said I guess your right. It probably will pop up eventually. Well honey how's your genesis project going? (David) Real good so far Heather. We not only found a couple of huge ice cavity's today, we already melted all of them and put oxygen and water all over the surface of Venus in the form of snow. You know Heather something suddenly hit me, since photosynthesis takes Carbon Dioxide and turns it into oxygen and a carbohydrate is only sugar and we already created snow all over the surface. Well I guess what I'm saying is, are we making home made snow ice cream on Venus. Then David looked at Heather and started laughing. Heather gave David a sexy smile and said science sure can be appetizing. What do you say we have one more drink and go to your place and maybe eat some dinner and then have a couple more drinks. Then Heather started giggling and said maybe watch a movie or something. Then Heather gave another sexy smile and leaned in close to David and gave him a kiss on the lips. Then David started kissing Heather back and said you know that sounds like a fantastic ending to a long but lucky day. There were also some Powleens in the Red Star and they were sitting in the corner at a booth having a couple of drinks. They were going over the genesis with some of the people in the science department. Back over at Chuck's table where Lieutenant Parsons and her amigo Lieutenant Fisher were.

Chuck was asking Jenna if she would go out with him some time. Jenna said oh I don't know Lieutenant. Then she smiled at Chuck and said I just might. Jenna was looking at chuck with a comical but sexy look and said if you do it right. Everyone started laughing and were looking to chuck for a come back. Chuck starting grinning for he had a reputation for being a smooth operator and said would you be so kind to join me Me-lady on a very fun filled day of fun and games at my house tonight at 20 hundred hours where I will court you and we can watch a movie of some kind and maybe have a couple of drinks?

Then Jenna started giggling with the same funny but sexy look, she knew she could have some fun here and said, well Chuck, that was pretty good my man but what do you mean by a very fun filled day of fun and games? Then everyone said this is getting good and started laughing. Chuck gave a confident smile and said I was just getting started. Don't you remember I said I was going to court you. Then Jenna said a long oh, you did say you were going to court me.

Now I guess the question is what do you mean by the phase court me? Your not going to sue me are you? Then Chuck smiled first and then looked intent at Jenna with a cute but hansom demeanor an said, well Jenna I guess it means that I like you and I want to get to know you better. I will do anything I can to please you or make you happy so we can have a good time on our date. Then everyone at the table said yeah now it's really getting good. Then Jenna said, wow you are a smooth operator. Ok mister smoothie, I will go on a date with you but if you try any funny stuff, I will punish you. Then Chuck started laughing and said I give you my word Me-Lady. Then everyone shouted he did it. Alright, way to go chuck, you pulled it off. Then chuck said what do you say we make the date two days from now after we get over all of the time consuming stuff on the genesis project?

Then Jenna gave Chuck a sexy but respectful smile and said what all do you want to do? Then Chuck said well I thought maybe we might just have a couple of drinks and maybe watch an old pirate movie or some other kind of movie what ever you want and just talk normal maybe play some cards or something joke around a little bit. No practical jokes though, I promise. Then Jenna said you know you really are a smooth operator and smiled at Chuck an gave him a quick kiss on the lips. Ok, how about two days from now on Thursday at 20 hundred hours? Chuck looked adventurous and said I will count the hours Lieutenant.

David and Heather started walking toward the door to leave and Lieutenant Courtney stood up and said everybody lets toast to Commander Braymer and his genesis project. Then everyone stood up even the Powleens and they raised there glasses and said this toast is for you Commander Braymer. Then everybody took a drink and shouted hip hip, hurray. Then David started laughing and told everyone thank you and Heather and David went ahead and left to go to David's Place. When they arrived David made him and Heather a couple of drinks and they sat down in the living room in front of the 80 inch TV monitor. David ask Heather if she might want to watch an old pirate movie. Heather said you know I use to watch that pirate movie that was a big hit in the early 2000 years. It was called Pirates of the Caribbean.

What do you say we watch that one? David replied I know that one. That's a good choice, a very creative movie. Computer look up and play the Pirate movie called Pirates of The Caribbean. (Computer) Affirmative. About 30 seconds later on came the movie Pirates of the Caribbean. They watched the movie for a little while and had another drink and one thing lead to another and they wound up in David's bed. They made love for about an hour and then they were so tired they fell fast asleep. They both slept good the whole night and before you knew it, the alarm came on and it was Led Zeppelin singing the song "Stairway to Heaven". David and Heather woke up smiling at each other and then started kissing again then David said well honey how did you sleep last night? Then Heather gave David another kiss and told him a night with you in the heavens and then smiled a little more and said was like a trip through the heavens on a magic carpet ride. Then David said, Heather do you mind if we don't make love this morning? It's just that, then Heather interrupted David and said I know you are so anxious to get on the bridge. Its ok honey we can have fun making up for lost time later. Then David and Heather got up and got dress. David was dressed in no time at all. So he ordered breakfast for him and Heather. He had it all ready before Heather was done getting dressed. The Aurora had a food processor that was in Earth translation called a deatomizer. What it did was create a molecule formula from a certain meal on the list of foods it can make. It would reproduce atom, genetic structures and then it duplicated it in the oven cooked. But fortunately we haven't been able to send live animals or people through it yet. But it was perfect for creating food. The Aurora was a Powleen ship and it was their technology.

It was on the ship when they traded. When Heather came out of the restroom and seen that David had breakfast all set up at the table. Hey, that looks good. Thank you honey I didn't expect this. David answered oh that's ok baby. You do the same for me all the time. I was just trying to return the favor honey. Then Heather said, you sure did baby, then Heather gave David a kiss and sat down at the table. They both ate a pretty good breakfast and then they gave each other another kiss and David left to the bridge and a couple of minutes later Heather took off to her office. She was an officers aid and worked in the Information department. She was a ship's consultant and a office secretary aid where ever needed and very good at what she did. Her department section was as big as a four story building on board the Aurora. They aided the entire ship when someone needed somebody.

David hurried to the bridge to check his data. He had thought about the experiment all night off and on. He thought he had a pretty good plan of attack. David arrived about 10 minutes earlier than normal. Most everyone always arrives at around 0600. David started turning on all of his station and his 30 inch monitor. David was going over all of the stats. Then said hey that's different. Oh my god the core temperature has cooled a lot more than I thought it would. It's because of the long eclipse. If this keeps dropping, oh my god we should be able to pull it off easy. I knew there would be a temperature drop but I had no Idea it would drop this much. At this rate of temperature drop, if this keeps up, we could have the right core temperature for the experiment in about three hours that's perfect for the experiment. Also looky here volcanic activity has reduced down to a minimal amount.

Man this is all looking better than I thought it would. We could launch all of the photosynthesis applicators and then we can do the experiment. This is looking very positive. Wait what's this? There is some kind of magnetic plasma energy on the surface. Maybe its some kind of a reaction from the rapid cooling from the eclipse, like static electricity. It seems to be increasing in size and strength. It is getting really powerful.

VENUS SHOWS HER LOVE

Chapter 6

I WONDER WHAT in the world is causing that? Then suddenly the bridge door opened and in walked most of the bridge crew. Then Commander Craft second in command walked in. You could see the Admiral coming down the hall talking with someone when the bridge door opens. Then David said good morning to everyone and then said good morning to Commander Craft. Then Commander Craft said to David, you got here pretty early this morning. Couldn't wait could you? Then David smiled and said you know your right sir. I couldn't stop thinking about the genesis experiment all night. I was up off and on for about three hours.

Commander Craft asked, have you come up with anything new? Yes sir David replied, as a matter of fact I have. Commander here's the latest, sir because we have had the planet eclipsed for so long. The inner core temperature has decreased by about 50% in just 15 hours by my calculations it will be at the perfect core temperature in approximately 3.5 hours sir. Then suddenly in walked Admiral Benson. Well hello everybody how is everyone this beautiful solar day. Everyone laughed and said that we're great sir. Everyone wished the Admiral a good morning back. Then Commander Braymer said good morning sir. I am ready to brief you if you are ready sir? Sure Commander the Admiral replied. What's our plan of attack. David answered, well sir first of all. Science engineering is going to launch about 78 photosynthesis satellite applicators. That will take about four and a half to five hours. Then sir I was telling Commander Craft before you walked in that when I first started this morning. I noticed two very important things and that is, one, the good news is because the planet Venus has been eclipsed so long that the inner planet core has cooled at an alarming rate but good for us sir. In fact sir, if it keeps falling at it's current rate, the core temperature will be perfect for the experiment in about 3.5 hours. Then the Admiral said what's the bad news Commander? Sir David replied, the bad news is, I have located some kind of a magnetic plasma energy mass and it is growing in size and strength and I do not no why sir. Why do you call it bad news Commander the Admiral asked? David answered, well sir, I guess because of a couple of characteristics. One being the intensity of the plasma energy and the fact that it is growing in strength. Two is that I do not understand the origin and how it is growing in strength, It is not making any since sir. It just suddenly appeared out of no where and seems to be generating its own energy. I have no idea what's making it happen. It could be some kind of reaction from the rapid cooling.

Or it could either be a bad electrical storm on the surface of some kind or maybe one of our canisters on the surface has a leak and there is a bad chemical reaction from it. There's one more thing sir. The average surface temperature has bottomed out from the eclipse and is now steady at -140F. degrees sir. Normally the surface temperature is right around 460C degrees sir because of all of the Carbon Dioxide in the atmosphere. But since we have had Venus eclipsed the temperature is much colder sir. Then the Admiral said will the colder than normal temperature hurt us in anyway when we take away the eclipse? (David) Unknown sir. It shouldn't. I feel that the sun would normally heat the planet back up very quickly in about one month but the difference is that when we take away the eclipse, the planets chemistry will be entirely different. But we can adjust the density of the eclipse.

Hopefully without all of the Carbon Dioxide and I know there will be a lot more Nitrogen, we just might see magic. We are also showing a lot more Oxygen too, which should mix well with the nitrogen and keep the atmosphere and core temperature down and should keep the surface temperature down also. Another good point is the ecliptic satellites are adjustable to how much sun we want to let back in on the planets surface. We should be able to adjust the planets surface atmosphere by how much sun we let through the tint shield. If we fail to achieve our goal through the chemical mixture at lest we should be able to compensate with the control of the atmosphere with the satellites. Then the Admiral said I like that. So what ever happens, we should have some kind of success in the experiment, very good Commander. So Commander what do we do about the energy mass? (David) Well sir there really isn't much we can do but study the phenomenon. If anymore data comes up sir, I will tell you immediately.

So where's that leave us now Commander, the Admiral asked? Well sir David glanced down at his instruments and all of a sudden the energy mass started to diminish. Sir the energy mass just now is starting to dissipate. You mean its gone, asked the Admiral? It is now sir, David replied. It might have been some kind of static charge in the atmosphere sir. That's pretty common because of the extreme change of the temperatures. The only thing we can do is keep an eye out for it in the future. If it comes back we may have a problem. Hopefully it won't come back and hurt our genesis experiment sir. (Admiral) Very good Commander maybe we are having some luck go our way. Then David said sir. Then Lieutenant Courtney spoke up and said, Admiral the science department just told me to tell you Commander that we are now starting to launch the satellite applicators into the outer atmosphere. Sir I also thought it might be best to discharge all of the chemicals first. Then adjust the satellite tent shield density for the actual experiment. Then what, asked the Admiral? We just wait it out huh, and just let your magic potion do it's work, right Commander? David replied Yes sir. Then we take notes for about three solar days or maybe longer and then go from there and start from scratch all over again sir. I am glad that the magnetic plasma field disappeared. Sir also the cooling of the core temperature is stabilizing right where we want it sir. We do have one problem here, the inner core is so motionless the magnetic field is almost nonexistent. Planet Earths magnetic field is very strong because our inner core rotates rapidly.

Venus's inner core is almost stagnated and unresponsive that's why Venus has no magnetic field. If we could get the inner core to move, we would have a magnetic field. On Mars we hit the core with the microwave beam in the beginning of the turn before the wide bind inside the core and it worked perfect but on Venus because of the anomaly it just seems riskier. David had no idea what made that magnetic plasma field occurrence. Admiral I'm going to go over a few things first and then I will check with my science department and see what they say sir. The Admiral replied, very good Commander, keep me informed. (David) Yes sir. Suddenly Lieutenant Courtney spoke out loud and said Admiral we are receiving another communiqué from Mars sir. It's the ruler of Mars, Venal Bermish. Excellent Lieutenant patch him through to me the Admiral said. Yes sir the Lieutenant replied. Then Admiral Benson said, this is a great honor for me Venal. What can I do for you sir. Venal had to talk in a translator so the Aurora could understand him. Hello Admiral how is everyone on the Aurora?

We are doing great here Venal the Admiral replied, we are working on a genesis project on the planet Venus right now. How's Mars coming along? I hope everything is well. (Venal) Thanks to all of you we are doing wonderful. The reason why I contacted you is the genesis project you are presently working on. You see we are following your progress on the genesis here on Mars. One of my colleagues here is a scientist, his name in short is Barco. He says you are in great danger if you try to heat up the core for an magnetic field. He say's because of the anomaly. There is a danger of an huge explosion. He is also saying it takes a lot of a volatile process for energy to generate that type of plasma magnetic field. He say's you should proceed with everything except heating up the core. Then the Admiral said, Venal we appreciate your help and I will convey your message to some one I believe you know sir, my 1st Science Officer Commander David Braymer. Then Venal said, how can I forget about the savior of our world.

We are erecting an monument in the name of you and Commander Braymer and all of the people on the Aurora for helping us. We love being apart of this new solar system family. Admiral if we come up with anything else we will contact you promptly. Then Admiral Benson answered, we thank you for not only your help but the monument too sir. You are also welcome to contact us anytime you fill the need. If you ever have any problems please do not hesitate to ask for help sir. Venal then replied, thank you for your concern and good luck on your genesis. Then Venal said end the communiqué. Did you hear all of that Commander, the Admiral asked? David said yes sir, and I think we should respect the Martian scientist Barco and not heat up the core. Let me check with my science department staff and grab some lunch and I will get back to you sir and tell you what all we came up with in about an hour or two Admiral. The Admiral said very good Commander, keep me up dated. Then David said, yes sir and got up and went to his quarters to grab some lunch. As David was going to his quarters he ran into Captain Dopar in the hall by the air shuttle. Then David said out loud hey how's it going Captain? Pretty good sir.

Captain Dopar replied, I was going to grab something to eat. Then David said, that's what I was doing, would you like to join me Captain for lunch at my quarters? Captain Dopar said, sure if you don't mind the company. Then David said mind, it's an honor Captain. My place isn't far from here, I will have you back in no time. It didn't take them long to get there and before you knew it they were chowing down on some chicken casserole with mashed potato's and gravy. Captain Dopar said this is good what do you call this? Captain, David replied, we call this chicken casserole, one of my favorites also. Then the Captain said very good choice. A chicken is a bird that doesn't fly right (David) Yes it is. Captain how have you been doing?

What I mean is do you miss your home planet? Are you happy? Then Captain Dopar said, yes I do miss my planet. I have four more of your years left to serve before I can go home but I am happy. I really love space exploration.

Then David said do you have any family back on Sybon? Captain Dopar answered, no immediate family, some distant relatives. I joined the space fleet early in my life. I have been with my space fleet for about 22 of your years. When I finish my military service, my world will give me a home and high status in my local hometown. That sounds something like the way my Earth is replied David. I was a teacher before I became the first Science officer.

I loved teaching young adults but it seemed like I was meant to be a space cadet myself. When I was a child there were some who were kidding around and called me a space cadet from time to time. Then David started laughing. Then Captain Dopar said we play around too, when we are young. I have found that most of the time everyone is the same all over the galaxy. But every now and then you find a race of people like the Arcons and the Thracians that are totally carnivores.

They seem to developed differently than those worlds that are both vegetarian and meat eaters. I guess it's something to do with being carnivores. Then David said Captain Dopar it is always a pleasure to talk with a long time veteran space man about all of your space adventures. If you ever have a problem or just want someone to talk to please give me a call. I love talking about your space experiences.

David and Captain Dopar talked some more and went ahead and finished eating. David asked the Captain if he was heading to his science department? He said he was. The Captain has helped a lot with the entire project. It was Captain Dopar that developed the special adjustable tint shield on the ecliptic satellites for the solar eclipse.

David thanked the Captain and his colleagues for all of their help and said that all of the Powleens would get credit for all of there help with the genesis project. We love your people, David told Captain Dopar as they went to the science department. Suddenly back on the bridge another light started flashing on Lieutenants Courtney's communications panel. Sir we are receiving a communiqué from Earth. Its the President's office Admiral. They are advising you to go to your office and wait for another communiqué from the President in 20 minutes Admiral.

I will patch it through to you sir. Admiral Benson relied very good Lieutenant I am on my way right now. Commander Craft it's your bridge now. Commander Craft answered affirmative sir, and then the Admiral got up and hurried to his office. When the Admiral got set in his office Lieutenant Courtney patched the call through. (The President) Hello Admiral how's things going with all of you on the Aurora? Admiral Benson answered, real good sir. As you know we are knee deep in the Venus genesis. We are just about at a point to start the final experiment Mr. President but there is a lot of preparation involved. We are almost ready though sir. Then the President replied Admiral all of us down here on Earth are rooting for you. The reason why I called you today is Admiral as of 0800 tomorrow you will be the proud owner of 20 more Powleen ships, all fully equipped with light speed capability and we just finished putting the Martians shields and weapons on board all 20 ships. I also had them put light speed and the Martians shields and weapons onboard the three Lunar Base ships. There really incredible now each of the three sections of ship have independent light speed. Admiral Benson you now have 28 ships all with light speed capability in your fleet. They are also all indestructible now. We went from space pilgrims to having the most powerful ships in our known galaxy thanks to the Powleens and the Martians, I love it Admiral. We are also working on setting up the Martian shields on the planet Earth, that's right you heard me right Admiral, the entire planet will soon have the Martian shields. After we do Earth, we are going to do Sybon and Mars. Our Scientist figured out how to make it work. Now the only thing that can hurt our planet is possibly a giant meteor. Our scientist figured out believe it or not, they figured how to project the Martian shields on to another object like a ship or something else. There trying to figure out how to project it onto a large object like a planet or a Moon. These type of shields are totally air tight. Then the Admiral said we could use it to set up Moon and planet base stations too. This is all so incredible Mr. President. Now if anyone ever try's to destroy Earth we have a super ace in the hole. This is all so fantastic, Earth has leaped way advanced to any of my wildest dreams, in just one year, unbelievable. Thank you for telling me all of this Mr. President. It really brightened my day sir. I fill like it's my birthday or Christmas or something. I feel like celebrating.

Then the President said, well Admiral you deserve to celebrate every now and then. All of you out there in the heavens protect us and help us have peace and freedom. We lost over 10,000,000 people on Earth and in the heavens fighting last year in that damn war, but it could of been a lot worse. Admiral if it wasn't for your space fleet we could have been wiped out or worse enslaved by the Arcon world. The thought of that terrifies me just thinking about how it could have happened. Down on Earth it all seemed like a sci-fi movie or something. Well Admiral I'm going to go I just wanted to tell you about your new fleet. Admiral Benson replied, thanks for calling me Mr. President. You really brightened my day. Your welcome Admiral, the President said, good luck on your genesis too, Admiral. Admiral Benson answered, thank you sir. You have a wonderful day, end communiqué. Then the Admiral started thinking wow we have a fleet of 28 ships and they are all indestructible and I'm in command. Wow, life is great.

Now if we pull off this Venus genesis. That would be like icing on the cake. Back at the science department David and Captain Dopar and some of the others like Lieutenant Plant and Captain Freedman were going over everything possible connected to the genesis.

Then David was saying, yes it's what the Martian scientist Barco said and I believe he knows what he is talking about. (Captain Freedman) Commander why don't we just do what Barco said and leave the core alone for now. David replied, I think that's exactly what we are going to do. Why not play it safe Captain? Lieutenant Plant suddenly spoke out sir. We have the last of the satellite applicators ready for launch and only a few surface canisters left to launch. Then the Commander said I want to thank all of you for putting up with me. I know we have all worked long and hard on this one. I think everyone here knows Venus is not as easy as Mars was. I want to say something else, everyone here will get the credit for this genesis, not just me. It will go on our records and I will set up a patch for everyone for our uniforms. The crew of the Aurora will get a patch and everyone connected to the science department and the other two departments that assisted in all of these launches, will get a special patch too. We still have a ways to go but I do see the finish line here. Remember once we get done with what we are doing on this experiment. We have to start all over again until we can sustain life on Venus. Hopefully we wont have far to go when we are done with this project. Well lady's and gentleman I have to head back to the bridge. Everyone lets concentrate on finishing launching the rest of the canisters down to the surface and start launching all of the satellite applicators. Captain it's 13:00 hours, do you think we can get all of these canisters down on the surface and all of the satellite applicators in orbit and in position by 17:00 hours?

We should get pretty close sir, replied Lieutenant Plant. It all depends on how many of the surface probes that carry the canisters are malfunctioning. Or if we make any errors from all of the programming we have to do. After all there is a lot of work yet before us. Then David said, yes I know Lieutenant just do the best you can do without killing yourself. If we have to we will finish early and do the rest at 0800 in the morning, I'm going to go back to the bridge and get situated and get this show on the road. Captain are you headed back to the bridge too?

YOU CAN'T FIGHT DESTINY

Chapter 7

NO SIR, CAPTAIN Dopar replied. I was going to help with programming all of the satellites in the cargo bay. Then David said, you're a good man Captain Dopar. I will try to leave the bridge a little early and come down here and help everyone. But right now I have to go to the bridge. I will see everyone later, remember don't kill yourself. Just do what you can. Then David headed back to the bridge to give the Admiral an update on the experiment. David arrived back at the bridge, the Admiral gave him a anxious look and said, well Commander how are we doing on the genesis? Are we on schedule? Yes sir David answered, everyone in the cargo bay are busting there buns sir. They are almost done on the launching of all of the canisters but then they will have to launch 78 satellites tomorrow with all of the applicators before we can do the experiment. Admiral I am going to work here at my station for a little while and then go to my quarters to do some calculating on a few thing's, Then I was going to the cargo bay to help with the launching of all of the satellite applicators. Then I was going to call it a day and see you at about 0600 tomorrow morning, if that is alright with you sir? Also Admiral we should be able to implement the experiment if there are no problems tomorrow at about 1700 hours. That's fine Commander just keep me informed and I will see you in the morning at 0600. Then David worked at his station for about another hour and then off he went to his quarters. As David arrived at his home he noticed the door was partially open. When he walked in he seen Heather in a beautiful sexy outfit standing over the dinner table preparing a candle light dinner. That was a pretty sight to see after a long day. David walked over to Heather and gave her a big kiss and said you know you're the prettiest sight I have seen all day. Heather said thank you real sexy like and gave David another hug and kiss. Then they both ate a wonderful meal and had a couple of drinks. They did their usual sci-fi movie and headed for the sack. They were both really tired. They both went right to sleep and before you know it the alarm was sounding off with a song. This time it was the "Wizard of Oz" theme song. David woke up and said I like that song you picked. Heather told him that the Wizard of Oz was one of her favorite when she was a child.

David said me too. They gave each other a kiss, and then they both got up and got ready for work. This time Heather made breakfast.

Heather did not have to go to work until about an hour later than David. So she didn't mind making breakfast. Before you knew it David gave Heather a kiss and away he went to the bridge. He got to the bridge early. No one was their except the night shift with Commander Tice the bridge CO or Commanding Officer in charge and a light staff. When Commander Tice seen David he said, There he is the genesis man. You couldn't wait could you Commander? I can't wait either to start the genesis. Today this should be the day of all day's.

Then David laughed, you know your right. It was so hard to sleep last night. I didn't want to bother Heather but your right I am anxious. I can't wait to do this genesis because I know it will be better than it was. Then everyone started to arrive on the bridge and changing shifts. Everybody said there hello's and went to their stations for the day. Commander Tice left to go home and go to bed and Commander Craft took over until the Admiral would arrive. Mean while on the out skirts of our solar system, Sybon, Earth and Mar's routine was about to change for the worst. Our arch enemy the Arcons and their friends the

Thracians were rushing to catch Mars and Earth and also Sybon by total surprise. They were coming in a vast horde of war ships for the destruction, and to enslave and colonize Sybon Earth and Mars. They had plans to take over our solar system in a massive surprise attack.

There was an excess of 1000 war ships all stocked with troops and weapons. The Arcons had a more advanced weaponry and cloaking capability now. They were totally undetectable even on infcr red. Some how they figured out how to totally camouflage the radiation trails. They were completely invisible. Their plan was to surround Earth and Mars and Sybon, also all of our space fleet's. Then open fire with their new weapons and catch us by total surprise. One thing on Earths side is our new shields and the Martian weaponry but Earth could still be destroyed by a massive surprise first strike or take on a lot of damage if they were not careful. The leader of the invading fleet was an Arcon named Menok. They were a ruthless world. They were the type of people to where all they did was take and destroy and enslave and some times eat there prisoners from all of the worlds they encountered.

They were a pirate race. The Thracians were conquered by the Arcons hundreds of our years ago. Their planet was called Maldin. Thracians were on average about eight feet tall and had a dog and human mix like appearance from there shoulders up they were ugly looking. They had humanoid like body's but dog like heads and they were very muscular. They also had Dog like teeth but they were abdominally big. The Thracians were from the second planet from the star called Gamma Hydra, from the Constellation of Hydra the Dragon.

The Arcons were from the third planet from their star in that same solar system called Bejeon. They had conquered about ten other planets in other solar systems. The Arcons were our size but had a human and snake mix like head look to them and were very muscular.

They also had two very distinguishing looking fangs. They were poison but not deadly. Their bite could knock you out and make you very sick but normally no one died unless there were numerous bites on the victim. In there primitive feeding state they would bite their victims and then devour there body's whole like a snake. Their jaws would separate so they could eat large prey. They loved their food fresh and alive before they would eat. Both worlds were humanoid but they were strictly carnivores.

They did eat some of there captives but they did have their own menu of life forms that they preferred on their planet. Most of them were brought to the Arcons world from some where else. They didn't like vegetables at all though.

Menok and his invading force would all be in place in about 5 hours. Six of our ships are way out into space all over the galaxy. That left us with only 22 ships in our area. But they all had the Martian shields and weapons though. The Arcons and the Thracians sent another huge invasion force to Sybon. Sybon had a fleet strength of over two thousand ships but about half of them were all over the place in the universe. The Arcons were going all out to take over the entire universe. They didn't know about all of the science brake trough's we had. Like the Martian shields and weapons that Sybon and Earth have discovered and implemented. The Powleens already had the biggest space fleet in the universe but when they installed the Martian shields and the Martian weapons onboard, their ships had became indestructible. The Arcons might get lucky and destroy some of the Powleen ships from the element of surprise but hopefully not all of them. The Arcons also had no idea that we had the capability to shield a entire planet or project the shields around other large objects like spaceships. Eventually though the Powleens were going to catch on that they were being invaded and put on all of their shields. Then there would be hell to pay. But how many people will die in the mean time.

They knew about the planet base Martian weapons from the last war but they didn't know about how far we've come with them.

The Arcons only chance to win is to totally surprise everyone with a massive first strike and wiping everybody out.

Back on Menok's bridge, Menok was going over the invasion with all of his Men. (Menok) Dabol you need to check with all of the Kima group. I don't want anyone to ruin the attack. If anyone messes up this chance for glory, I will wipe out their family name on our planet Bejeon. I do not want anyone to fire until I give my command. (Dabol) Yes Menok, it will be done by your rule. We will annihilate all their men and enslave their women and eat all of their children. Then Menok looked intent at Dabol and said I even bet they are tasty too. Then they started laughing and watching the view screen of them coming up to the outskirts of Pluto. Then Menok got on his communicator and said to all of his invading force. Listen up this is Menok. I want everyone to wait for my word to fire. I want everyone to check in when you are in your positions. I want Demins fleet to totally surround Earth first, I will take the smaller fleet to surround Mars. I want all other ships looking for all of their ships and as soon as possible, I want them in position because we will have to wait on all of you. Now lets do it now. Then all of his fleet started to split up and go their own direction, all of them totally invisible. They all had a kind of feeding frenzy look on their faces. They were a very carnivorous race of people.

Meanwhile back on the Bridge of the Aurora everybody was totally unaware of their on coming fate. David was just coming through the bridge doors. The Admiral was anxious to get started on the genesis project. Then the Admiral said, there's the man of the hour. Well Commander is everybody organized and ready to get under way? David answered yes sir, engineering and maintenance, also a lot of people from the science department are just about done with launching all of the surface canisters and they are also going to start programming and launching all of the 78 satellite applicators. Hopefully by four and a half hours from now. They have been busting their buns down in the main cargo bay sir. I am so proud of them and all of you on the bridge too for your patience. If we pull this off, we will yet have another planet to colonize. That is so fantastic just saying it.

(Admiral Benson) Very good Commander. I can see your on this Commander. What do you need us to do on the bridge? David replied, well sir there really isn't anything for us to do on the bridge at the moment sir. I guess we just wait and do other things until they get all of the satellite applicators launched. That will take a good four or five hours sir. I will be checking all of my data on the genesis while we wait. David went hard at it for about 2 hours at his station and decided to go to the cargo bay and see if he could help everyone launch the rest of the satellite applicators. David told the Admiral what he was doing and went to the cargo bay. As he arrived he noticed everyone working hard. David then walked over to where Captain Dopar and Captain Freedman were. over in one area of the cargo bay. Then Captain Freedman said, there he is. David replied I see everybody is busting their ass down here. I thought I would come down and help with the satellites. How far are we along? Captain Freedman spoke up. We have had a little bit of luck. We have already launched 42 satellites and we have 36 satellites left to launch sir. Wow, you guy's have been kicking ass. How can I help? Well sir, you can start over here on these 15 satellites. The instructions are over here sir. We are almost done with these two and we will come over and start helping you Commander.

What we are doing is programming the satellites first. Then we let maintenance charge the applicators with the photosynthesis mixer. Then the cargo bay staff over there launches the satellites. David said hey, you all have this down to a tee. Let me go get situated and get started. You guy's are doing a great job. Then the Commander went over and started on the satellites. They were programming away. It wasn't long until Captain Dopar and Captain Freedman were done with what they were doing and came right over and started helping David.

One after another they were cooking. They finished the set of fifteen they were on and went to the last set of fifteen satellites. Finally about two more hours and they were on there last two satellites. David was working with Captain Dopar and Lieutenant Plant. They were just about done with their satellite and so was those on the other satellite.

David sounded out, well mine are done how are you guys coming along. Then Captain Dopar said we're about done now too sir. In fact we are done right now sir. Then they let the science department people start charging the last two satellites. It didn't take long to charge them and to launch them. Then David and Captain Dopar and Lieutenant Plant also Captain Freedman and a couple of men from maintenance went next door at the Red Star lounge to take a final break before going home. As they arrived the Commander said bar keep please set me and my friends up with what ever they want, this one is on me. Everyone was totally beat but they said alright. Then David said we finished way early. I never thought that we would get this far today.

You guy's just had everything so organized that it went so quick. Then Lieutenant Plant said I had one that just wouldn't cooperate with anything I was doing, it took forever to get it right. I must have programmed it ten times before it started working right. Then David said yeah I had one like that. What I did was disconnect the power and wait ten minutes. Then I rebooted before it worked for me. Boy this beer taste good. Well do you guy's think we should do the experiment now or wait until tomorrow? (Captain Freedman) Well sir, you know what I am going to do is go home and get something to eat and then drink a couple more drinks and then go fast to sleep. Its up to you Commander if you want to do the experiment or not. It will take three solar days to completely spray all of the mixture anyway and you will have two wait for the photosynthesis to start taking effect. That could take weeks. I only know one thing I will be out like a light in about one hour. Then Lieutenant Plant said yes sir me too. I just want to go and lay down, I'm so tired. Then David said I understand all of you have been working on these satellites for about two weeks now, I bet all of you are glad its almost done. They were sitting in a booth that had a port hole window and David was looking out and suddenly seen a flash of light over by Venus. Did you guy's see that? Everyone said no what?

I just seen a flash of light over there by Venus. I wonder what that was? I bet it was a reflection off of one of the satellites. Then Captain Dopar said that's probably what you seen sir. I seen a couple of flashes earlier about a half an hour ago. I just thought it was a satellite too. I don't know what else it might be without a probe. What they didn't know was it was four Arcon battle cruisers getting in position to open fire with all of their weapons in a surprise attack. They were just waiting for the order when all of their ships were in position. They still haven't found all of Earths ships yet. Then there was another flash of light, everyone seen that one. David said there it is again. Then Captain Dopar said yeah I seen it too. Then everyone else said they seen it too. I bet your right it must be a reflection off of one of the satellites. I wonder if there malfunctioning with a fire. Then David said you guy's go ahead and get some rest.

I'll check the satellites out just to see if there is a malfunction somewhere. Everyone had a couple more drinks and headed to their residence. Commander Braymer went ahead back to the cargo bay to check for a malfunctioning satellite but as he looked he did not find any malfunctions at all. David just blew it off as a reflection off of one of the satellites. Then he headed back to report to the Admiral on the bridge. As Commander Braymer arrived back at the bridge, the Admiral was waiting intently to find out if we were going to implement the genesis project today or not. Then David walked in through the bridge doors. Then the Admiral said hello there Commander your just the man I want to see. How's things going on the genesis project? David answered real good sir. Everyone from the science department and maintenance including me and Captain Dopar down in the cargo bay area has just completed launching all of the surface canisters and all of the satellite applicators. We just launched the last two ten minutes ago sir. We can either do the genesis now or wait till tomorrow morning sir.

What do you think is the best Commander, the Admiral ask? Well sir, David replied, all of the satellites are orbiting Venus. I guess it would be better if we implemented it now because the longer the satellites are orbiting the more chance we have for a malfunction sir.

The experiment will take about three solar days to complete sir. Because it takes about three days for all of the photosynthesis mixer to be dispensed. It's set up that way for a slow and gradually dispense.

Then we would have to wait for the photosynthesis to take effect and that could take up to two weeks or more sir. Then the Admiral said Commander that makes since to me. Can we do it all from the bridge Commander? Yes sir David replied. I can do it all at my station. The first thing I will do is set off the surface canisters, they held up well too sir. Then all I have to do is tell the satellites to commence application. Then we let the mixture do its thing for about three days why we take notes and then we adjust the satellite tent shield to a desired spot and go from there sir. Then the Admiral said it sounds like you've got it right to me Commander. This is all sounding so positive to me. Lets go ahead and do the genesis Commander. Then David said very good sir. The Admiral said, oh Commander, we have been seeing flashes of light is that connected to your satellites? David answered yes sir, we have seen the phenomenon too and all of us came to the same conclusion as you sir. All though we never launched a probe to find out what the flashes of light were.

I did check to see if there was a fire or malfunctions of any kind on any of the satellites and found none sir. Sir I am about to activate the surface canisters. Admiral the surface canister's are now activated sir. Admiral I am now activating the satellite applicators. Sir the Venus genesis experiment is now in progress. Admiral Benson said very good Commander, now all we have to do is wait, right Commander? Yes sir Admiral, David replied. Now's when all of our hard work hopefully will pay off. Everyone on the bridge was watching the main viewer screen.

TERROR IN THE HEAVENS

Chapter 8

THEN EVERYONE SEEN another flash of light right over the planet Venus. Then the Admiral said there it go's again Commander. (David) Yes sir, I seen it too. Let me check to see if there is a satellite in that area. Sir I don't see anything there on my screen. Then the Admiral said lets launch a probe Commander.

Then David said very good sir. Launching the probe now sir. The second he launched the probe you could see the probe shoot toward the area where the flashes of light were coming from. Then there was a distortion in the space and suddenly you could see a bright red light coming right at the Aurora. It was so fast we didn't have time to recognize what it was. The Admiral recognized what it was at the last second though and then it hit the ship and there was a massive explosion. Then two of the four Arcon ships decloaked one after another on two sides of the Aurora. The other two were on the other two sides, you just couldn't see them but they were there. Then they all opened fired on the Aurora with their new weapons. The Aurora was taking massive hits one after another. You could see huge sections of the Aurora get blown off into space. You could also see people floating off into space. The first hit was close to the bridge and it caused everyone on the bridge to get hurt and some were knock out and some dead but the Admiral was still conscious and yelled shields on, but Commander Tice was knocked totally out with a head injury and was in grave condition.

So as the ship just kept taking one hit after another it looked like the end for the Aurora. The Arcons new weapons just kept hammering the Aurora. It was horrifying. David was still conscious but hurt real bad. He heard the Admiral say shields up and it seemed like everyone that was still conscious seen that Commander Tice was hurt bad and everyone was trying to get to the weapons station to activate the shields. David was the closest and crawled over to Commander Tices station and then the Aurora started to lose gravity. Then David and everyone else started to float. The Aurora just kept getting bombarded with massive hits one after another. It seemed like the closer David got to Commander Tices station the more we would take another hit and he would be jolted away from Commander Tices station. With the help of God David managed to push off of his station and float toward Commander Tices station to just make it to push the button on the Commanders station console. Low and behold the shields came on and so did gravity. Then everyone who was hurt and everyone else that was floating fell to the floor hard. The Arcon fire was no longer a threat but the Aurora was almost destroyed. They just kept firing all of their weapons but they were useless now because of the Martian shields. You could still some what feel the ship getting hit by oncoming fire but it was minimal and was doing nothing to the ship.

Then suddenly the other two Arcon ships decloaked and you could see all four of the Arcon ships surrounding the Aurora trying to hammer away at our shields. They were firing all of their weapons but it was doing nothing. Then the Admiral crawled to his seat grasping his broken arm and tried his chair console Led control panel to fire all weapons, but it did not work. So then he pushed the communicator on his uniform and told the computer to connect him to the armament department and ordered them to fire all weapons but they reported back that they took some hard hits and there were body's everywhere and all weapons were down but shields were working good. They had many casualties and twice as many injury's all over the ship. Then everyone started helping all those who were down. David was helping Commander Tice and suddenly he past away in David's arms as the Admiral was watching. Then the Admiral got on the main computer and proceeded to tell everyone that they were just hit in a surprise attack by the Arcons but our shields were working and that those who could help the others to please start helping everyone and that we are safe so far from our shields. He also said that all those who can not move because of a injury to please wait for someone to come and help you. There will be someone there as soon as possible. Thank you and may God be with all of you. Mean while the Arcons just kept firing all of their weapons but it did nothing. Everyone still felt some of the pounding but it was not hurting the ship.

Everybody that was able started getting situated at their station and doing system checks. Everyone was taking all of the injured to the hospital's by the thousands. Lieutenant Fisher was critically injured and they were taking her to the Hospital. There was massive damage all over the Aurora. They couldn't fire back, they were helpless until weapons were back online. The Arcons couldn't figure out why they couldn't blow the Aurora away and were getting more angry. Back on Earth there were hundreds of Arcon and Thracian ships orbiting earth cloaked and they started pounding the surface of Earth and Mars. One of the first thing they targeted was both of the big Martian guns. Earth was getting bombarded by the Arcons new weapons. It was horrible, millions of people dying at the blink of an eye. They were attacking all of the major city's, millions of people dying all over the world. Earth had a population of over twenty billion people, but not anymore. They lost over eight billion people in the first strike along. The Earth looked doomed if they didn't get the shields up soon. The invading force just wouldn't stop bombarding Earth with their new weapons until it started to look hopeless. All of the people everywhere were dying. Everyone thought they were goners until everyone got their shields turned on. It was incredible all of the enemy ships just kept trying to wipe out earth but when they put there shields on, the invading fleet was helpless when it came to their offensive. They were really frustrated, they couldn't do anything. But they were ordered not to stop firing their weapons and they didn't, but it was useless. Earth and Mars took a lot of damage and a lot of casualties before they could get their shields up. Mars was almost wiped-out. Earth lost 14 of their ships and the rest were heavily damaged, only the lucky ones saved themselves with their shields. The new Martian shields have saved everyone. Earth and Mars and the Powleens were starting to target all of the invading ships that were still firing at the shields. Then Earth and Mars was starting to launch all of their ground aircraft. Earth lost both of the Martian big guns but still had some of there ships that still had weapons. One after another the Martian weapons were destroying the invading fleet. They had also put the Martian shields and weapons on a lot of their surface aircraft. They just kept destroying one enemy ship after another, all the enemy ships that were caught inside the shields to close to Earth. The enemy ships caught outside of the shields could not penetrate the shields and when they tried they exploded on impact. On Sybon it was all out war too.

They were in the middle of celebrating one of their holidays and the Arcons caught just about everyone on Sybon by total surprise. They were almost destroyed. The Powleens lost a lot of their ships too.

They also had a lot of casualties into the billions but eventually was able to activate their new shields like everyone else and then they started blowing away all of the invading forces. They were cleaning house. When the Powleens figured out what was happening they sent some ships, what ever was available close to our area to help Earth and Mars. It was so easy with the Martian weapons. One after another the Powleens were destroying the enemy ships. The Aurora wanted to help Earth but engines and weapons at the time were down for the count. There were a lot of casualties and injuries. Everyone on the bridge had some kind of an injury and there were deaths and missing persons being reported all over the ship. They were almost destroyed.

Everybody in engineering that was not hurt that bad was franticly trying to repair computer problems and help get help for everyone and the armament division was doing everything they could to repair weapons but they took a direct hit without shields. It almost killed everyone in the armament section at the time. There were only a hand full that was up and around but they were hurt too. From head injury's to broken arms and legs. Because of the Martian shields everybody was able to get to everyone to save them and take them to the hospital's. There were two hospitals, one in the middle of the upper half of the ship and one in the middle of the lower half of the ship. The hospitals were strategically located on the Aurora, they were in the safest place onboard. The hospital's were getting packed. It seemed like half the ship was hurt and some very bad. There was one surgery after another. The Arcons just wouldn't stop firing their weapons though but it was useless. Admiral Benson broke his arm and leg but it did not hinder him, he couldn't wait for weapons to be repaired. He wanted some pay back. David had a slight head injury and he also had a broken arm and a hurt leg but he was still helping everyone he could.

Lieutenant Fisher did not look good she was critically injured and so was Ensign Brian Baker the son of Admiral baker from the Kawaka ship. David and Lieutenant Courtney helped with Lieutenant Fisher and everyone else on the bridge. David was so angry and so was everyone else. Everyone wanted them weapons back on line. The Arcons would not stop firing there weapons even though it was doing nothing but making everyone want them weapons back online so they could wipe them out. Admiral Benson ordered more technical help to help the armament division, they were hit hard and he also wanted to get weapons back as soon as possible. All he kept thinking was, he hoped they didn't leave before he could get weapons up. Finally the armament communiqués the bridge and said they might have the Martian weapons up momentarily in about fifteen minutes but did not know how long it would work. Communications were also down, they just had internal ship communications. Everyone just kept helping all that they could. About 20 minutes went by and then Captain Welch contacted the bridge and told Admiral Benson, we have enough juice to fire the Martian weapon once about every fifteen minutes, until we get the main reactor back on line and that will take a day or two. Then the Admiral replied that's ok Captain when can we start firing the weapon?

Then Captain Welch said you can start now sir. Then the Admiral said with a mean like tone. Thank you Captain I owe you one.

Then he turned to Lieutenant Parsons and said Lieutenant lock on to that larger Arcon ship and fire the Martian weapon on my mark. Then the Lieutenant said sir we are locked in now. Then everyone was looking intently at the view screen and the Admiral said blow that evil bastard away Lieutenant. Lieutenant Parsons said I'm honored sir and fired the weapon. The red beam hit it's target and three seconds later the massive Arcon ship exploded into a burst of flames. The explosion was so great because everyone was so close, it blew all of the ships back in space a short distance. Everyone's shields held up though.

Immediately after the Arcon ship exploded the other three Arcon ships that were left returned back to the Aurora and started firing all of their weapons again but to their surprise it did no damage what so ever. Then the Admiral communiqués the armament and told Captain Welch to contact the bridge every time we can fire our weapons. The Admiral's left arm had a compound fracture, you could see the bone pushing through the skin. He was in a lot of pain from his leg also and he was so mad he had red in his eye's. Then the Admiral received another call from the armament and gave the ok for another attack. The Admiral wasted no time and told Lieutenant Parsons to lock on to another ship and fire on my mark. The Lieutenant said locked on Admiral. Admiral Benson gritted his teeth and said blow them snakes away Lieutenant. The Lieutenant looked intently at the Admiral and said its my pleasure sir and fired the weapon and three seconds later that Arcon ship exploded.

The last two Arcon ships just kept regrouping and then they would fire all of their weapons but it was doing nothing. Then suddenly Captain Welch communiqués the Admiral and said sir we have a bad wiring problem down here and we are starting to have some trouble with the Martian shields. We do not know how long they will work sir.

Then the Admiral said to Captain Welch, Captain I know you are doing everything you can but please don't stop, do everything you can to keep them shields up or were done for. Captain Welch was also hurt bad and told the Admiral that he would keep at it and that he would not stop and also said Admiral weapons just went down again.

Admiral we are losing shields too. Shields will be down in 2 minutes sir. Then the Admiral said just do the best you can, don't worry about weapons Captain just please keep them shields up because if you don't we through. Things did not look good again for the people on the Aurora. About a minute and a half went by and the Admiral receive another call from Captain Welch and told the Captain that they had a burn out with the breaker box and he could not stop the shields from going down any second. Then Captain Welch said sir we just lost shields and then the Admiral said well I guess we should say our prayers Captain. Suddenly the Aurora took one more hit in the engine compartment and then it stopped. Then the Admiral passed out cold and David took the helm. Captain Welch said sir we have shields but I do not know how. Then David said thank God. Suddenly four Powleen ships decloaked and open fired on the last two Arcon ships right when the Aurora lost it's shields.

THE END OF A NIGHTMARE

Chapter 9

THE POWLEENS PROJECTED their shields onto the Aurora and finally both of the Arcon ships were destroyed by the Martian weapons on board the Powleen ships. Then Commander Braymer said to Captain Welch don't worry Captain our problems are over, the Powleens are here! Take care of yourself Captain its all over now. I will note your heroism. Then all of a sudden communications came back online. Then Commander Braymer opened ship to ship communications with the Powleen ships and very graciously thanked them. Then the Powleens sent a lot of helpers over to the Aurora to help out with the injury's. Commander Braymer put himself on the entire ship telecom and reassured everyone that help will be coming to you so try to hang on and that the nightmare is almost all over. We have been saved by our friends the Powleens. Then everybody cheered. Then David said lets take care of our dead and wounded.

There were twenty or more Powleen shuttles starting to board the Aurora. The Powleens were truly angels from heaven.

Then David started to help with the Admiral and everyone on the bridge. He wanted to hurry so he could go and check on Heather to see if she was alright.

David had a broken arm and a head injury but he was going to be alright. David finished up with helping everyone on the bridge and rushed to the air shuttle so he could go to Heathers place first and see if she was there. If she wasn't there, then he would try her main office. David was trying to get all the way to Heathers place on the shuttle.

Suddenly the shuttle started to slow and then came to a stop. You could see how the Aurora had big sections of the ship just blown away. David got out of the shuttle and their was a major standing close by looking out to the heavens and David walked over to him and started to ask him where everyone was. For all of the decks one through six were blown out into space. The Majors name was Major Loggins. He was just standing there with a very sad look on his face and he looked like he may have been crying. David looked closer and said can I help you in anyway. The Major replied no sir. I'm afraid its to late for helping me, them snake bastards killed my whole family. My wife and two sons. Then David said oh my god I am so sorry. Is there anything I can do for you Major.

The Major replied with a sad look on his face no Commander I will be alright. You wouldn't happen to know where everyone is going that survived, do you? Then Major Loggins turned and looked up at David and said I heard that there were some people gathering in the big auditorium and at the air ramp lobby and most at the hospitals.

Then David said why don't you come with me and we can look for you family too. There's always a chance that some of your family survived the attack. The Major replied I was talking with my wife with my communicator when they attacked. Everyone was home. I am just going to stay here for a while and then come and check everywhere else. David felt sorry for the Major but he had to go and look for Heather. He told the Major to take care of himself. Then he told him how much we needed his help right now and that he would look for his family because he felt there's always a chance that somebody got away before they attacked. But he had to go look for Heather. The Major told David that he had to go by foot from here on out because the air shuttle was gone from this point on. Then David thanked him and went on to Heathers office on foot it was about a two mile walk. David arrived at Heathers office and no one knew where she was. Then one of Heathers friends, Specialist officer Stefanie Nicks walked over to David and said, Heather did tell me she was eventually going to look in the laundry department for her blue dress again. Then David said your right I remember her talking about going one more time and look for her dress there. David said thank you to Specialist Nicks and rushed over to the laundry department. He had to go there on foot too. As he was getting close to the laundry department he noticed that they had taken a direct hit right next door. He ran in, and the laundry room was all destroyed and their was laundry everywhere. He started looking in all of the rooms and did not find anyone. That's when he started to worry.

David started talking to himself saying, God Heather, I hope your alive somewhere. There were boxes and all kinds of laundry everywhere. Then David seen another couple of rooms in the back and called Heathers name out loud but there was no return voice. Then David started to lose hope and then he heard some kind of noise in the back. When he rushed in the room he seen something move under all of the laundry and boxes. He went over and started to uncover who ever was under all of the debris. To David's amazement it was Heather that popped her head out of all the laundry. She was holding her blue dress in her hand.

Heather looked at David and held up the blue dress with her hair looking all fluffed up and said I told you I would find my blue dress. Then David said Heather your alive and started to laugh with joy.

I've been looking everywhere for you. I was starting to give up hope and here you are. Are you all right honey? Then Heather called out to David with a look on her like she had been in hell and back. I think I am ok honey but man that was really something. One minute I here explosions the next minute we lose gravity and then we get it back and everything fell on me. David started laughing and gave her another big hug and said I'm am so glad your ok. You know I love you don't you? Heather smiled and then David pulled her out from under all of the debris. It wasn't easy because of David's broken arm. Then Heather grabbed David and said your hurt let me help you out honey.

David asked Heather if there was anybody else in here now? Then Heather said I don't know David. David and Heather looked around some and did not find anyone. Then Heather said huh, I wonder why nobody looked for me and then fixed the sling on David's arm and they both went to the hospital. Heather had a couple of bumps and bruises but she was alright. Then David looked at Heather and smiled and said, I am so glad you are alright and what ever you do don't lose that blue dress again. You know that dress saved your life. Then there was a pause and David looked at Heather and said you know I love you right. Then Heather said with a smile, yes I do and I love you too David and they kissed intently. Then David ask, Heather will you marry me?

Heather looked shocked that David ask her that but she soon came back to reality and said with a sexy smile on her face, yes I will. Then they hugged and kissed very caringly. Then they walked into the hospital doors. Back on earth they were trying something new. The Arcons were tapping into our satellites orbiting the Earth above the shields and were going to send a deadly audio virus beam through the airways. You could see them shoot a beam at one of the main communication satellites that went through the satellite television network. Everyone that was watching their television's suddenly went into some kind of a coma or they were very sick. As soon as Earth caught on they shut down all of the satellite network system's. Then the Arcons started blowing away all of the satellites. There were a lot of civilians hurt. Casualty's were up in the billions, all over the world. Major city's were practically obliterated all over the world also.

Moscow and New York all wiped out to the ground and many other cities everywhere else. Mars only had one small city and one being built. Just about everything they built was destroyed except for the place where they had the Arcon and Thracian prisoners. It was the only thing that had the shields working. Also a lot of the Martians that we resurrected were killed. When the Arcons attacked Mars everyone on Mars was taking lessons on how to fly the 800 Martian fighter crafts. They were so easy to fly they were fun to drive. They made a major difference in the war on Mars. Once Mars got it's planetary shields on it was all gravy after that. Soon after that the Powleens started to arrive in hordes on the scene destroying the Arcons and their forces. It only took the Powleens about a day and a half to get to everyone everywhere. But they were angels from heaven. With the Martian weapons the Arcons were defenseless against them and one after another the Powleens were destroying the Enemy fleet. The

Arcons still out numbered everyone about 100 to one but they were not able to do anymore damage because of our shields. They were just wasting their time until someone was able to get to them to blow them away. All of the Arcon and Thracian ships that didn't explode fell into Mars and Earth's land base shields around the planet and then exploded. The Arcons must have had the order to fight to the death because they didn't stop firing, but it was hopeless. The Powleens were not hurt that bad. They lost a lot of people and a lot of their fleet. But they had so many ships out in deep space that when all of the trouble started they started reporting in and they still had well over 1000 ships.

Not all of the Powleen ships had the Martian shields and the weapons though and when the Powleens finally got into the battle it was devastating to the Arcon and Thracian invading armada.

Everywhere all over the universe the Powleens where getting pay back. All of the Powleen Moon ships had over one thousand weapons on there ship. If they had the Martian weapons on board most of the out going fire would be the Martian lasers, not all of the Powleens had time to put the Martian weapons and shields on board their ship yet. The ships that had the lasers were being surrounded by ten or more ships and the Powleens could coordinate the fire to all of the individual surrounding ships at the same time with the special Martian laser. The Arcons did not know which of the ships had the weapon and which did not. They thought all of the Powleen ships had the weapon's on board.

Twenty of the Powleen Moon ships were like a thousand of the Arcon ships because of them being untouchable with the Martian shields. The Powleens would just let them accumulate in numbers until there were a lot of them firing on them. Then they would open up with all of he Martian lasers on there ship's. It was a spectacular sight to see all of the enemy ships were exploding like pop corn popping on the campfire. They would target multiple targets at the same time with the Martian laser's. It was devastating to the evading Arcon and Thracian fleet. They didn't know what hit them. The Powleens were taking 20 to 30 ships out at one time. It was a spectacular sight to see. Eventually Sybon organized and invading force and sent them to Bejeon and Maldin. The Arcons and the Thracians home planets, in the constellation of Hydra the Dragon. They bombarded their two planets for 3 day's straight and caused so much damage it set them back into a primitive past in their solar system. They could have easily destroyed the Arcons and the Thracians. The Arcons made there own fate with all of there evil deeds. They really weren't going to hurt anybody anymore for a very long time now. Back on the Aurora just after they were attacked everyone was getting help for all of their injuries. The President on Earth sent the Admiral another Moon-ship to have. They were still going to have to transfer all of his crew onto their new Aurora because the old Aurora was to badly damaged. They were still going to repair her and get it back into action. But she had to be put in a special space dock. But it was going to take a lot of time because she was so damaged. The Powleens only have six of the big repair stations but they also had light speed. The Powleens needed most of their repair stations because of the war but they let us use one. You could repair them without the repair stations but it sure was easier when you could use one though. There were two of the Powleen ships that were with the Aurora one of them was like the Kawaka style ship and the other was another Moon ship like the Aurora. The Powleens not only saved the people on board the Aurora but was also helping all of the critically wounded in their hospitals on their ships. They also helped saved Earth and Mars. All three planets were like in a brother hood now from all of these wars in the last couple of years with the Arcons and the Thracians. We now have a federation of planets. One thing for sure though if we hadn't went into space we would never of had all of our advances that we have achieved. We would probably have been wiped out by the Arcons when they first attacked us.

Admiral Benson was already recuperating from his broken arm with his new cast. Just about everyone that was onboard either had a cast on their arm or leg or head patches or some kind of injury if they were one of the lucky ones. Our new Aurora was coming anytime now and then we will all change ships and get our homes back. Lieutenant Fisher was recovering from surgery and was serious but stable now and she was expected to fully recover but be in a wheel chair for the rest of her life. We were having one funeral after another from all of the people that had died on the Aurora.

Everyone was so sad about losing either a close relative or some of their friends. David never did find Major Loggin's family because they were all killed from the first initial strike just like the Major thought. Many good people died that day.

Everyone everywhere would probably be cheering right now if it wasn't for all of the dead and injured. There was a lot of cheering at first when the war was over and the Arcons were on the run. Until everyone seen all of the damage and all of the casualty's. Then finally the Aurora's replacement ship arrived three weeks after the first initial attack and everyone that was able started moving over to the new Aurora. Most of all of the Moon-ships the Powleens made, had a certain design and were pretty much identical to all of the others. They did have some that were customized but most were the same.

Everyone's home's were where they were before on the original Aurora. So most people just moved back to the same location. The hospitals were in the same location on both ships. The hospitals on the original Aurora were still in great shape because of their location, being in the middle of the ship was a good design. The hospitals were about the only thing that wasn't effected from the Arcon assault. One thing for sure is if it wasn't for the Powleens we would have been wiped out.

We could not have taken anymore hits. After a couple of days of everyone moving to the new Aurora Admiral Benson gave the orders to start moving all of the patients over to the new ship all except the critically hurt. It would take a good two weeks to get everyone moved anyway, maybe even longer because of all of the wounded. The Admiral didn't want to detain the Powleens very long. We really did appreciate their help and the Admiral thought they may have more important things to do. Maybe even going to help their own people.

The Admiral really valued the Powleens. They were heaven sent. David and Heather finally got situated in there new places. This ship was even newer than the one we had before.

It had so many more extras. David had his arm in a cast. His arm was broken right above the elbow. He was getting around pretty good though. The Admiral requested from Earth if the President wanted the Aurora to come to Earth and help. The President said that they had everything under control there and that it would be better if the Aurora took care of it's self and to get transferred to their new ship. The Admiral also told the President how the Powleens saved all of the people on the Aurora and what had happened during the attack. The Venus genesis had to take a back seat to everything else. No one even spoke of the Venus genesis project. Even David had went through so much in the last three weeks, that he even forgot about the genesis project too. Now that David has transferred to the new ship with a broken arm he will have a chance to concentrate more on the genesis project. They have been so busy with all of the funerals David and Heather have went too. So much sadness. They usually do bury in space quite often. But because of the death toll, there were too many.

Now with light speed it was not really that much of a problem to bring the body's back to Earth for their family's for final funeral services. We have a couple of supply ships that have light speed capability that travels everywhere to take supplies to everyone. That's when they would pick up any deceased body's that have been kept on ice to take back home to Earth if requested. After the Powleens helped with the transfer of the new Aurora ship, they were going to take all of the Aurora casualties to Earth. Everyone was still very sad. There were 4200 deceased shipmates going back to Earth. Their were two casualty's on the bridge, one was Commander Richard Tice and the other was Ensign Brian Baker who was Admiral Bakers son. Ensign Baker died of a severe head injury in the very first assault. If we hadn't lost gravity a lot more people would have died on the Aurora that day.

Admiral Baker is the Commanding Officer in charge of the first Kawaka ship that the Powleens traded us. He arrived yesterday and took his son back to Earth to his family for funeral services. He was a broken man, it was like he lost a part of himself. He also took about 500 other body's back to Earth, as many as he could take with him for others. Everyone had a feeling in the back of their minds of shock and vulnerability and hurt. The whole war only lasted two and a half of Earth's solar weeks, yet it was so devastating to everyone. We thought we were so secure with the Martian weapons and shields. That just goes to show you when you think you're at your safest you can be, it may be just the opposite. I think that's why everybody was so stunned. We were still not done counting all of the dead on Earth, Mars and Sybon. Back in David's quarters, David was watching his new television monitor, it was showing pictures and talking about all of the devastation from the War. David thought to himself, man I can't believe how much damage the Arcons were able to do in two day's from the initial attack. Them evil bastards. I know in my heart that the heavens are a whole lot better off without them snake sons of bitches. Maybe we should go back and wipe them out for good, so they can't regroup.

The Powleens said they sent them back into their stone age. I hope that's exactly what they did. Maybe I have to distance myself from this so I can get on with my life. The Powleens have a saying, we all make our own destiny and they are always saying stuff like," Our minds are our souls and when we are out of the normal you are endanger of losing your soul or your mind". So try to get back to your normal way of things as soon as possible. You know maybe that's what I am going to do. Why don't I get back to my Venus genesis. I don't think anyone has checked up on the genesis. That's it then, that's what I will do to get my mind off of them damn Arcons Sons of Bitches.

VENUS COMES TO LIFE

Chapter 10

COMPUTER, TURN ON the view screen and focus on the planet Venus and give me the up to date data on the Venus genesis project.(Computer) Affirmative. Then the view screen went from the news on T.V. to the prettiest site of Venus you ever will see.

It looked like Venus was still covered with snow and ice. To David's amazement the ecliptic satellites were still in tact and working perfect, as he was checking out all of the Data. Ok then all of the canisters are empty and the satellite applicators have long been done. We are ready to adjust the satellite tint shield. We should be able to adjust the tint in about 3 to 5 hours. Wait what's that?

Oh no, the plasma energy field is back and it is stronger than it was before. Computer zoom in on the planet Venus's surface where the plasma energy field is. Lets see if we can see this bad boy while it is visible. Affirmative. Then the computer started to move it's viewer screen and then you could see it focusing on a certain area and then suddenly you could see where the energy field was coming from. Then David said what the hell is that. Computer, zoom in more. (Computer) Affirmative. Then the computer zoomed in real close. Oh my God, what the heck is this. This looks like some kind of alien construction. David just kept looking at the phenomenon. It looks like some kind of a geothermal set up. But for what?

Then suddenly the plasma energy field started to dissipate, and soon it was gone again. Wow, I love a mystery. Computer I want you to analyze the anomaly on the planets surface and tell me what it is. The Computer replied, affirmative. Working. The anomaly is the source of the magnetic plasma energy field.

Function unknown. Confirm terrestrial in origin, origin unknown. Computer why would some alien race construct this structure? (Computer) Working, construction is probable for geothermal power source for large ship or Power source for small city. Computer how old is this device?

(Computer) Working. Insufficient data. Date of origin unknown. Computer are we go for final adjustment of the satellite tint shield for the Venus genesis. (Computer) Working. Affirmative.

Computer at what time would be the best time to adjust the ecliptic satellite tint shield for maximum effect on the genesis project?

(Computer) Working. You can adjust the density of the tint on the satellites at any time. The experiment is ready for completion. Excellent. This couldn't look any better. I can't believe that we are still a go on this genesis after all that we went through. The Arcons must not have viewed the satellites as a threat. Computer is there a pattern to how often the plasma energy field is activated? (Computer) Affirmative. The anomaly is occurring precisely every 100 minutes.

Computer connect me with Admiral Benson. Affirmative. Then Admiral Benson answered. Hello Commander what can I do for you? Hello Admiral how's that arm and leg feeling? Oh I guess as good as to be expected replied the Admiral. I am still trying to get back fillings in some places. How's everything with you Commander? David answered well Admiral it is so hard to do anything with one arm in a cast. That's the only thing that's bothering me, you should see me. I am getting pretty comical. Admiral the reason why I called you is I found something on Venus I think you need to know about sir. I also wanted to update you on the Venus genesis. The Admiral answered go ahead Commander, let me have it. David then said, sir if you turn on your view monitor, I would like you to zoom in on a location L1S8 on the Venus screen layout sir. Ok Commander give me a second here. Ok here we are. You could hear the Admiral say what the hell is this. What exactly are we looking at here Commander? What is that object commander? Admiral you are looking at our magnetic plasma energy field sir. I have been analyzing the data with the computer and Admiral it appears to be some kind of ancient geothermal energy source for either a city or a large base or a large ship of some kind sir. This is all just speculation at this point. One more thing

Admiral, it gives off a lot of energy every 100 minutes sir like clock work. Then the Admiral said are you sure Commander? I am just speculating on the origin and the function sir but the first initial findings are indicating what I'm saying sir, David replied. The Computer confirmed it Admiral. Also sir believe it or not all of the genesis experiment is still intact and we can adjust the satellites at any time sir. Wow Commander, I'm sorry I have been involved in a lot of sadness in the last couple of days.

I have only been on our new bridge once since I have been on board. I have been so busy moving from ship to ship. Oh I understand sir I am the same way here David replied. I just now started checking up on the Venus genesis in my quarters to take my mind off all of the negative. When I found that the anomaly of the magnetic energy field was back for a few minutes and then it went away again like before but I was able to zoom in on it to get these pictures. Thanks to our new computer on board our new ship sir. Then the Admiral said very good Commander that's a good idea, I mean to take your mind off all of the negative stuff and concentrate on the genesis. Well what do you say me and you meet on the new Aurora bridge in about 3 and a half hours from now. I do not know who is on the bridge right now but lets say we find out in about three and half hours from now Commander. You know Commander maybe everyone hearing about the Venus genesis project might take their minds off all of the negative like you say Commander.

Maybe it will make everyone fill a little better inside. Then David answered, That sounds great to me too sir. I will see you then sir.

Then the Admiral said computer end Communiqué. David hasn't seen very much of Heather in the last couple of days except for funerals. One of Heather's hidden talents is in the officer's aid or secretarial aid and also a form of officer's administration consultants.

She was a very busy woman at present. Now David was going to concentrate his thought back to the genesis project. Then David started thinking, Maybe because of all of the problems. You know what, I'm not going to bother anyone. Besides I really don't need anyone's help at present anyway. I will just meet the Admiral on the bridge in about three and half hours. Right now I guess I could do some more studying. David was going over some of the data from the Venus genesis when suddenly he looked over by the dinner table and he could see a light sparkling in a gold smoke looking cloud with tiny sparkles all through the smoke like area about the size of a large dog. David said what the Hell is that. Then David said Computer connect me to Admiral Benson at once. Then the Admiral said hello, David replied sir, I am sorry to bug you but I felt it was important. Then the Admiral said your fine Commander what's the problem? Sir I want you to look over my shoulder and see what's in my living room. Then David moved out of the way and the Admiral said, yes I see it. What is that Commander?

Well sir, I do not know, it just appeared right in front of me two minutes ago.

Then It moved over from the table to the sofa where I was sitting. Then David said did you see that? Yes I do the Admiral replied. David focused into the cloud like phenomenon into the gold light source. David moved his hand toward the light to touch it. Then David's hand started to glow with a gold tint. Then suddenly as quick as it appeared it disappeared. Well, what do you think of that Admiral.

Is your hand ok Commander, the Admiral asked? Yes sir, David answered. I feel surprisingly better than normal. Is there anyway I can get you to get checked out before we do the genesis on the bridge.

Admiral I really feel good. What ever is was, it is gone now sir. Then the Admiral said ok then but if you have any reaction at all to that anomaly, I want you to immediately go to the hospital, alright Commander? Yes sir David replied. Then the Admiral said you know Commander. If I didn't know better I would have to say, that looked like an extraterrestrial entity, or a intelligent life form. I agree Admiral David replied, I felt something when I touched it. I do not know why but I felt like it was not only friendly but don't ask me why but it felt highly intelligent. I had such a feeling of peace come over me. Admiral don't think I am going crazy but I believe it wants me to go to the structure on the surface. Then the Admiral said what makes you say that Commander. David answered, I don't know sir. It is just one of the feelings that came over me when I touched it. Commander I would like you to go to the hospital and get checked out ASAP. I just want to know all of the facts, like maybe they can tell us what kind of a chemistry make up that cloud was from your hand. Or something entirely different. But we do need to know all of the facts Commander.

The Admiral laughed and said you never know It could be contagious or something. I am not going to make this an order. But I think you should go get checked out. Then David replied Admiral I will go get looked at in about 15 minutes sir. Then the Admiral said Commander I always said you were a good man. Also don't worry if it takes a little more time than normal. I mean about our meeting in about 3 hours. Just give me a call and let me know if your going to be running late. Yes sir, David answered. I will keep you informed. Then David said end communiqué. David was looking at the view screen when he seen the anomaly come on again. There's that energy field again. Computer zoom in on the base of the structure at maximum zoom. (Computer) Working. Then the zoom started and David said hey that's pretty close. What is that? It looks like an information plaque.

Computer focus on that label on the base of the structure. Then suddenly you could see writing on the tablet. Computer analyze the data on the tablet and tell me what language it is and then translate.(Computer) Working. The language is Hebrew and it translates into "The Eye Of God". Does it give a date or any other data.

(Computer) Working. Yes there is more Data, but I can not read because writing is to small to zoom in. Then David said Computer turn off the view screen. Then David got up and finished getting dressed and off he went to get his check up. When David arrived at the hospital it was super busy. They were taking care of all of the patients and moving in from the other Aurora. But the new Aurora was already well stocked. The first thing David said was boy I have a feeling this might take longer than I thought. Then David walked over to Dr. Moon and started to tell him what had happened and that the Admiral wanted him to go get checked out and to have his hand analyzed to see if there was any foreign substance's still on him. To see if we could possibly get analyzed and identify what it was. Then Dr. Moon said that's quit a story Commander. Lets take an x-ray and also swab your hand and send it to the lab which was just next door and just to see what we can find. I love a good mystery. They took there test and it didn't take long for the results to come back and Dr. Moon came over to David and proceeded to tale him what they have found. Well Commander we have the results back and your not going to believe what we found on your hand. Then David gave a funny look and said what did you find on my hand? Then Dr. Moon replied well first of all your all right and second of all we found traces of real gold on your hand Commander. Then Dr. Moon started laughing and said what did you do find a gold mine on Venus or something? Then David looked stunned and said wait till the Admiral hear's this. He's never going to let me hear the end of this. Then David said Thanks a lot Doctor but what do you think that thing was? I don't know what the hell that was Commander but if you have gold all over your hands from touching it. I might go touch it again and again till I can go and pay off all of my debt. Your health is fine Commander in fact it's better than most, except for your broken arm and all. Then David started laughing and said you know maybe your right and got up and said thanks Doc and headed out the door for the bridge. When he arrived it was still a little early for the meeting with the Admiral. So he just went over to his station and Captain Dopar was their filling in the spot of science Officer. There were three seats at David's station.

Captain Dopar was an excellent science officer and a good assistant. In fact he could run any science department by himself because of his knowledge in science. As David walked up, David said hey there's my favorite Powleen. How are you doing Captain? He looks over at David with his long neck, I am doing well Commander. I was just monitoring the planet Venus and the anomaly on the surface sir. It is initiating an energy charge every 100 minutes to the second Commander and seems to be alien in origin. Then David said their's more Captain a lot more let me fill you in before the Admiral comes to the bridge in about one hour. David proceeded to tell Captain Dopar everything he had experienced in his quarters. Captain Dopar was mystified about the story and then we were getting reports of sightings all over the ship. David also told him about the inscription that was on the base of the anomaly and the fact that it was very old and in the Hebrew Language. Then David said you know Captain we have been looking for years for information of what our ancient language was for our history. This is proof that the Hebrew language was our first basic language through out the galaxy or at least in our solar system. Then Captain Dopar said this is all very interesting. We still search for our ancestry or origin in our area around Sybon and beyond. In our history we found out that about 40,000 of your years ago we just seem to have appear out of nowhere. We have no idea where we are from. Or how we got there. Then suddenly in walked Admiral Benson. The Admiral seen David and said there he is. How you doing Commander? I mean what did the hospital say Commander? Well sir David said, your not going to believe me but do you know what they found on my hands? Then the Admiral said they found something. What did they find? Then David looked at him with a straight face and said Gold flakes sir, very tiny gold flakes. Then the Admiral started laughing and said your kidding me right. You had real gold on you ? Then David answered yes sir, and now we are getting reports of sightings all over the ship. The sightings are happening in conjunction with the energy field. Every time the energy field comes on everyone starts seeing ghosts. Also sir I tried to zoom in on the inscription on the plaque at the base of the structure. I could only make out some of it but we could not zoom in enough to read all of it sir. But what we could see was in Hebrew and it translated into "The Eye Of God". I think we should organize a landing party for that one function, to read the rest of the inscription sir. Maybe we will find something else Admiral.

Then the Admiral said do you think we should do that before we finish the genesis Commander? Sir David said it would probably be better to do it now sir because when you have high temperature you will always have high pressure and when you have low temperature you will always have low pressure. You see Admiral normally the pressure on the planet would be to high on the surface. We would implode on the surface. But since we eclipsed the planet we now have a very low pressure because we have very low temperatures all over the planet Venus. Do you understand what I am saying sir? Yes I do Commander, the Admiral replied, your just saying because we have the planet eclipsed we have low pressure on the surface and we should be able to be alright on our expedition. Sure Commander I will approve the landing party but everyone wear their air suits and take no chances, Ok Commander? Then David said, very good sir. I will organize a landing party and I will keep you informed Admiral. Then David asked Captain Dopar if he wanted to join him on the expedition. Captain Dopar was honored to participate. David told Captain Dopar that he would get a couple of men from security to go with them on the expedition. Everyone was in agreement and started planning the project. They decided to go in two hours. Then everyone went to prepare the project in the science department. The cargo bay was preparing a shuttle for a launch to the surface of Venus. David couldn't wait to read the inscription on the structure. They were all to meet in the

Red Star lounge that was right by the shuttle bay lobby. Then they were going to suit up and then load onto the shuttle. It was really cold on the surface but the barometric pressure was a little higher than should be but it was acceptable. They had suits that could with stand absolute zero with no problem. Everyone was right on time and they had a couple of drinks and off they went. The shuttle launched and down to the surface they went. As they slowed close to the surface the magnetic plasma field shot high into the Venus sky. You could see a golden greenish cloud with blue lighting inside of the cloud. It did just like before just like clock work. Then David instructed the pilot to stay on the out side of the cloud and rotate downward to the surface. Then suddenly the field was gone. Then David said ok we should be alright lets sway back to the south and see if we can find a good spot to land by the base of the structure. Then the shuttle veered back toward the base of the structure and came in as pretty as could be and low and behold there was a great spot right in front of the structure.

There was a problem though, they did not for see the wind. The wind was about 30 to 50 miles an hour but right at the base of the structure it was so abnormally calm. So the shuttle set down right in front of the structure. Then everyone readied for the first walk on the surface of Venus. Then David said to everyone you know all of you are making history today because no one has ever set foot on Venus before.

So I hope you are ready to go down in history. Everyone said wow I never thought of that. Then everybody was ready to set foot on Venus. David swung open the shuttle door and they were literally 10 feet from the structure then David walked over to the plaque on the base of the structure and immediately took a picture of the writings on the wall and they looked around a little but found nothing else. So they went ahead and loaded back up and lifted off pretty as can be and off they went back to the Aurora. As they approached the Aurora it was quite a sight to see. You had the Powleens Kawaka ship next to the Powleens Moon ship next to our new Aurora Moon ship next to our old Aurora Moon ship. On are return we almost couldn't figure out which ship was our ship. Also on our approach we flanked the old Aurora real slow and got a first hand look at all of the damage. It was really something when you were seeing it from looking on the outside of the ship in space. We also took a lot of pictures of the hull. That's when everyone on board of the shuttle realized how lucky the survivors were on the old Aurora. There were huge chunks of the ship just blown out into space. It looked like a giant meteor shower had it the Aurora. They were going to do a video documentary of the damage on the Aurora and a damage report for the President with all of the video. Then finally we circled around and we approached our new Aurora. You could see the bay doors starting to open as we approached and then we pulled into the cargo bay and sat down as easy as could be. Finally the bay doors closed behind us and we started to unload in the cargo bay lobby. We were going to the Red Star Lounge to go over everything that we seen because everyone had to fill out reports on the mission to hand in and then David was going to his office in the science department to analyze and translate the alien plaque into english and share his findings with everyone else in his department. When David arrived he could see that just about everyone was retracting all of the satellites that had the applicators on them. They were busy as bees. David went ahead and took his camera to his office and downloaded all of the pictures he took from the surface onto his computer.

When he got to the picture of the plaque with all of the writing on it, he then translated the language using his computer. On the final draft the computer printed out the translation of the message that was on the base of the huge structure. When David started reading the translation his jaw dropped and said no way. He read some more and said again with a little longer tone, no way. Are you telling me this is a time machine?

THE EYE OF GOD

Chapter II

NO WAY, I can't believe what I am reading. I can't wait to tell the Admiral this one. He's going to flip. Wait a minute, if it still works we can go back in time and change the past. We could save all of the people that died. We can change everything. We can turn all of the shields on before they hit us in the surprise attack. We can wipe them out before they can hurt us.

Wow. I can't believe this. As soon as David realized what he had he immediately communiqués the Admiral. The Admiral answers and say's, how's everything. Well Commander I can't wait to find out what you found. David had a serious look and said Admiral as soon as I realized what I had I contacted you immediately. Man from looking at your face, you've found something big haven't you? Oh boy sir, I found something I know your going to like. Here goes Admiral. Sir the structure is a time machine of some kind. The ships computer has translated the inscription on the tablet sir. Admiral if we can figure out how it works we can go back in time. Sir we can have everybody put on their shields right before the Arcons attack. We will change our destiny and save ourselves from the Arcon invasion. Take a look at these pictures and the translation sir. We may be able to save billions of people from that damn war sir and change our fate

Admiral. Then the Admiral said this is unbelievable Commander. How do we find out how it works in our life time? Unsure sir their must be something else on the structure we didn't see. Something different. We have to go back down again on another expedition Admiral and do a better search sir. Maybe if we are at the base at the time the plasma field engages. Sir I have to do some more studying and I will get back to you hopefully with some options. Then the Admiral said lets go for safety first Commander. This all sounds so fantastic Commander but if we can pull off going back in time and changing the out come of that damn war, I'm all for that so please keep me in formed. Then David said I will sir. I will get back to you before 1700 hours sir and then David said end communiqué. David got back on his computer and then told all of his staff what was going on and everyone was so hipped up and hoping for a miracle. In the end though they had to go back to the structure. David was watching the anomaly engage on the surface and took some temperature readings at the base from a small probe that they left at the base and it did appear to be ok, right in front of the structure where we were parked. Then David remembered the wind and how abnormally calm it was right in front of the structure where they were parked. It all seemed so mystical some how. Also every time the plasma field engages everyone on all four ships starts seeing strange sightings on board their ships. There's got to be something else we didn't see. I guess that's it then, we need to do another expedition. Then David got on his computer communiqué intercom in the science department and ask for four volunteers for a another Venus expedition. Then Captain Dopar and Captain Freedman and also Lieutenant Plant and Ensign Beck all came forward. Many others wanted to come but we couldn't all go. David told everyone that he was going to contact the Admiral and set this up for the next time the plasma field engages in about 94 minutes so everyone ready yourself for another expedition. We will probably meet in docking bay number ten in about two hours. I'm going to my office and I will meet you in the docking bay in two hours then. Then David hurried to his office to contact the Admiral. It was way earlier than 17 hundred hours but we need to get on this so we can finish the Venus genesis.

Computer contact Admiral Benson. (Computer) Working. Then you could here the Admiral, hello Commander how's it going? What did you come up with? Well Admiral David replied, we have a pretty good plan of attack sir. Admiral I was wanting to launch another expedition in about an hour and a half sir. It would be me and Captain Dopar and Captain Freedman and also Lieutenant Plant and Ensign Beck. We were going to meet in docking bay ten sir. Also we left a probe on the surface at the base of the structure and I was watching it in my office. The probe indicated that it would be alright, in front of the structure sir. Then the Admiral said, ok Commander you know me I will go along with you because we have been pretty lucky up to this point. All I ask is safety first Commander. I'll be watching from up here. I hope you figure it out Commander, good luck. Then the Admiral said end communiqué. David studied the structure some more and did some more calculations and ate some lunch and before he knew it, it was time to go to the shuttle bay. Well David said the only way to find out anything is to go look some more at the structure. So David got up and went to the docking bay to meet everyone. He arrived a couple of minutes early and went into the Red Star lounge for a quick drink. The Red Star was right next door to the docking bay number ten.

He could see everyone getting off the air shuttle and walking towards the Red Star or the docking bay. David hurried and finished his drink and went out of the lounge doors towards the docking bay to meet them outside. Everyone seen David walking towards them and said there he is over there. When David walked up, he said is everyone ready to go on a magic carpet ride and smiled. Everyone chuckled and said, yes sir. What do you say we go ahead and board shuttle number ten. As everyone was starting to board, the shuttle Captain greeted them at the door with a smile on his face, saying next stop Venus. His name was Captain Stark. He was a really experienced shuttle pilot. Everybody hurried and sat down and got buckled in and before you knew it you could hear Captain Stark say Aurora this is shuttle Moon Beam requesting permission to depart to the surface of Venus. Then you could here, shuttle Moon Beam, permission granted for departure.

Then you could feel the shuttle pull away and the Cargo bay doors opening and off they went from the Aurora down to the surface of Venus. You could also see the last of the satellites from the genesis experiment returning to the docking bay for final return. Everyone was looking out the shuttle windows and descending at a rapid rate and before we knew it, we were circling the base of the structure for our landing zone an sat down as pretty as can be. We had 30 minutes before the magnetic plasma field would engage. That was just enough time to look the base over some more for more writings or some clue to the answers to the time travel device. Everyone unloaded off the shuttle Moon Beam. Then David said, there's got to be something that stands out so everyone spread out and lets check this baby out. Lets look for anything out of the ordinary, especially around the base. Then everyone took off in their own direction all around the structure. It was very hot but they went over it with a fine tooth comb. Still no one found anything. Then David said we have eight minutes until the plasma field engages. Maybe something will reveal itself to us at that point in time. I only know that the probes said it was safe from the shuttle to over there by that big rock when the field engages. That was just that one time too. I mean I am not trying to scare you but I think we should play it safe like the Admiral said and sit inside the shuttle while the field is engaged. I know that you are all in suits but to minimize risk, I will be the only one out side of the shuttle taking readings and I know you will be taking readings inside of the shuttle also. I Just want to be out here so I can get a birds eye view.

I might have to act quickly, so you can watch me and if I need help, if its safe, you can come an rescue me, ok? Then everybody agreed with David and they all got back into the shuttle and there were two minutes left before the field energizes. Then David said standing in front of the sliding door on the shuttle. I am going to be right over there in that little clearing. We will still be communicating so if you people see something I don't from your angle, please do not hesitate to tell me immediately. Remember if it isn't safe stay inside the shuttle. That's an order! Then David shut the shuttle door and went over to the clearing by the base on the structure. There was only 45 seconds left before the plasma field was going to initiate the field. David was ready with his analyzer in his hand. Then finally 10, 9, 8, 7, 6, 5, 4, 3, 2, 1 and then you heard a loud electrical humming sound and behold the plasma field engaged. One thing David didn't count on was the magnitude of how much power the magnetic field had. It was pulling David closer and closer to the structure. Everyone inside almost got out to helped David but when it got to a certain point it was pretty quick. When he reached a certain distance from the base you could see a golden beam shootout from the structure and hit David. It lasted about 5 minutes and just like clock work the magnetic plasma field was off again. There was David clasped at the base of the structure, out cold. He was glowing a faint gold color too. His eye's were sparkling gold also. Everyone ran to him and put him on the shuttle as quick as they could. They rushed him back to the Aurora where everybody was waiting with a stretcher to take him to the hospital. He was barely breathing and had a faint pulse.

But he was alive. When they finally got to him, they were able to stabilize his vital signs. He was in a severe state of coma. It did not look good for David. The Admiral seen the whole thing on the view monitor and was terrified. So did the everyone on the bridge and everyone on Earth, Mars and Sybon and some that were watching in the science department. The Admiral notified Heather about what had happened and she rushed to the hospital to be there by David's side.

She stayed with him all the while and about twelve hours later finally he started to come out of his coma. Heather was half asleep when she looked at his blanket and it started to move and then she focused on David's face and suddenly his eye's started to open. The first thing David did was turn to Heather and said hello honey, what's wrong and then David looked around and realized where he was and his memory came back.

Heather gave David a big hug and a kiss and said I knew you would come back to me. There's no way I was going to let you get away this easy. Then she gave a sexy smile and leaned in again and gave David another kiss and she got up and grabbed David's call button and in came a nurse and Dr. Moon. Then he seemed like he was normal at this point and everyone was happy. But suddenly his eye's started to turn sparkling gold and David's face became emotionless and blank. But his eye's just shined away. Almost like a dim light bulb. He just kept laying their and Heather started to panic before Dr. Moon calmed her down, then everyone went to work on David. David was not responding. All of his vitals were normal, he was just none responsive.

Then finally David came out of it again. Dr. Moon said looky here and David's eyes started clearing and looked normal again. David started to get responsive again and came back to the living. There was no more recurrences and after a while David was looking and acting like himself again and all of his vitals were better than normal. All most to good to be true, his health was perfect now even his broken arm was totally healed. So Dr. Moon Released him from the hospital and put him on a couple of days of bed rest and relaxation. Heather was so relieved and took David straight home for some rest and something to eat. She was going to stay at David's home for a couple of day's so she could keep an eye on him. Heather fixed David a dinner for a king and pampered him with love. Before you knew it, David was off to sleep.

He slept for a good six hours before he woke up and Heather was right there by his side asleep. Then she awoke and seen that David was awake and said good morning honey how are you feeling? Then David smiled and replied I feel great but I don't seem to remember what happened. Then Heather said honey you were struck by that energy field and then you when into a coma and your eye's turned a funny looking gold color and scared the hell out of everyone. Also the Admiral has been calling about every 2 hours to see if you are ok. I remember now. Wow Heather it was weird, I don't remember getting zapped but it was like I went to another world. I just kept having these weird dreams. There was this presence there that was glowing a bright gold color. Please don't think I am crazy but I think it was God. Then Heather said man that was quit a dream. If it was God David, I think he saved your life. Then Heather leaned into get close to David and gave him an intimate kiss. David do you think you will be alright while I run to my office and take care of a few things.

David answered yes sweetheart, I will be fine, I feel great. So go ahead and do what ever you have to. I will just be here watching T.V, ok and David kissed Heather again. Ok David I will be back in about two hours tops. If you start feeling funny call me at my office, alright baby. Then David said, ok but I will be fine don't worry. Then Heather got ready and rushed to her office. After Heather left, David put on the video of the expedition to watch what happened to him on the surface. As he was watching the video he realized that it was almost time for the plasma field to engage. In fact the field was about four and a half minutes away from engaging. David told the computer to focus on the alien structure. David reached down to pick up his coffee and accidentally knocked it on the floor and spilt it everywhere. Then David got upset and looked at the cup and suddenly, it crushed itself.

David looked confused and said how in the hell did I do that? Then the computer told David that the structure would engage it's field in 1minute and counting. Then an LED display came on the monitor for David to watch. Then finally the field engaged.

David immediately collapsed on the floor and is eye's turned gold again and this time there was a gold aura surrounding David. He stayed like that until Heather came home from her office about two and a half hours later and she called the hospital for help. Heather felt so bad because she didn't stay with David. He had slipped back into a coma. Everyone was working hard to help David and finally they had him stabilized again. The next day David woke up and felt great again and realized where he was and Heather was asleep in a chair next to his bed. David arises out of bed quietly so he doesn't wake up Heather, then he gently grabs her and puts her in David's bed. She was so tired she didn't know what David did and she was sleeping like a baby. Then David looked at his Doctors chart at the end of the bed. David said to himself, wow it happened again. Then David remembered what he did to his coffee cup and that it was precisely before the magnetic field came on. David walked over to the computer monitor at the doctors desk station. Then he typed into the key board, and asked when was the next engagement of the magnetic plasma field. Then on the monitor, the computer print out started typing the answer. They still used the keyboards in the hospitals because doctors do not want the patients to hear all of their diagnoses.

(Computer print out) Magnetic plasma field will engage in 10 minutes and 46 seconds. Then David turned off the computer monitor and walked back over to his bed and laid down with Heather and laid her head on his shoulder. David was starting to worry about the field engaging again. Then suddenly Heather was starting to wake up and she opened her eye's and thought she was in David's bed at his home.

She looked over at David and David looked at her and they kissed. As she was kissing David she started roaming her eye's around the room and then she suddenly remembered what happened and said a long whaaat. Then she looked David in the eye's and said your alright, I was so worried about you. I should have never have left you. David made the sound of sssss, it's ok honey it's not your fault at all. I may not have a lot of time but I have to tell you real quick what's going on honey. You she every time the plasma field engages, it seems to put me in a coma. I just checked with the computer and the magnetic plasma field is going to engage again in about 3 minutes. Then Heather said oh no. Did you tell Dr. Moon this. No, I hadn't had the chance yet honey. I just woke up about five minutes ago. Heather got up and went over to the other side of the bed and pushed the call button. Then Dr. Moon and two nurses came in and Heather preceded to tell the doctor what David told her, and Dr. Moon walked over to the computer and turned on the monitor and ask the computer when the next time the Plasma field would engage. The computer typed out, plasma field will engage in one minute and 23 seconds. Dr. Moon order the nurses to ready some medication just in case David were to slip back into a coma. The nurse ran and prepared the injection and then Dr. Moon said be ready with the injection. Then sure enough when the field came on David went back into a coma. The nurse gave David the injection and the heart monitor became stable again. David came out of his coma and smiled and started to talk and his voice was a lot more deeper now. Even David looked at Heather kind of weird because of his new voice.

Then David said with a deep voice, I know now what I should do. Then Heather said what honey, what do you have to do? Then David sat up in bed and moved his legs over the edge of the bed and started to get up and Dr. Moon said wait a minute sir, you can not get up. We need to run some more test. Then David said with that deep voice. No Doctor there is something I have to do for everyone. All of a sudden the Admiral walked into the hospital to see if David was alright.

Then he seen David sitting up on his bed and walked over to everyone to say hello. Heather grabbed the Admirals arm and said sir maybe you can talk to David we can't seem to get him to listen. He keeps on saying that he knows what to do now and he keeps on trying to get out of bed. Then the Admiral looked at David and said Commander what is it you feel you have to do? You know what we have to do is what ever your doctor says. Then David began to talk to the Admiral with his new voice, I have to go back down to the structure sir. The Admiral looked at him kind of funny because of his voice and the Admiral remember what they were talking about, how to activate the time machine. Then the Admiral looked at Dr. Moon and said doctor why is his voice so deep now? We're not sure Admiral. Yes Commander I hear you, but you did not find anything down there when you went. Oh yes I did sir, David replied in his new deep voice. When I got zapped it activated the time machine through me. I believe I have the power to make it happen now sir. How are you going to do that Commander, the Admiral asked. David answered with his new deep voice and said Admiral I really do not know how to explain this, I just know you are just going to have to trust me sir. Admiral I have to go back to the structure on the planet at the very next time the field energizes. I am fine now. Admiral I have a chance to save billions of people. I have to try sir. Commander I can not allow you to just kill yourself the Admiral replied. What if your wrong? Then David said sir I am not wrong sir. Admiral you can see for yourself that the structure seems to be on and functioning in me. Just look at what it is doing to me. I may not have a choice. That is why I have to go through with this.

Then Dr. Moon spoke up and told the Admiral that he didn't know how long we can keep bringing David back from his coma state.

So far we have been pretty lucky. I still do not know why this keeps happening to Commander Braymer. But I have a lot of people on this including the lab on some brain scans we are waiting on. Some outside force keeps affecting Commander Braymer and it does seem to be coming from the plasma energy field on the surface of the planet.

Because of the simple fact that every time the field engages David goes into a coma that could kill him. I do not know for sure but maybe the Commander should play this out even though it could kill him. The reason why I am saying this is because I do not know how much more the Commander's body can take. If we do nothing the plasma field could kill him after the next couple of engagements. It is going to engage another five times before this day is out. We have to do something if we can? I do not know what other side effect the Commander will have if we wait to long. Admiral the more I think about it the more I recommend letting the Commander finish what he feels he has to do. Then the Admiral gave a funning look and said to David, Commander I guess because of current circumstances I am going to give you permission but how are we going to know what to do at the right time, like to put our shields on if you are able to take us back in time? I mean how are we going to know what to do in another time zone, when we are in this time zone. How are we going to project what to do in another time zone, especially if you get your self killed.

Then David said we will have to alert not just Earth, but Sybon and Mars and all of our ships everywhere. I am hoping that my memory will stay intact. But I will put some other security in place just in case.

But Admiral I do think I should be down on the surface the next time the plasma field engages. I just don't believe I will survive the night if I do not face this problem. Who knows maybe I will be able to fix our problems. Then the Admiral said Ok then, we have one hour and twenty minutes before the next field engagement to plan the next expedition. Commander I guess your right. It does look like you are going to have to do this. Be sure to lets us know what to do about the time displacement or we've done it all in vein. Ok sir, David replied in his deep voice. I will not let you down sir. I know you will do your best Commander, the Admiral answered. But even you can make a mistake.

I do not want anybody else to die if they do not have too. I have gone to way to many funerals lately. Then David said yes sir. I'm with you on that one. Let me get dressed and prepare for this expedition and I will head to the shuttle bay and get this over with.

Then David got up and got dressed, as he was getting dressed everyone noticed the bed that he was laying on. It was shining from all of the tiny gold particle's on the bed. The doctor giggled a little and said look at that Commander, everything he touch's turns to gold.

David laughed out loud in his new deep voice and everyone looked at him with worry. Then David looked at everyone and said don't worry about me. I will be fine you'll see. Then David left the hospital with Heather. First they went to his quarters to go over some data on his computer. He was feeling very weak but he was determined to see this through. Heather made him a sandwich and a fruit drink and sat down with him. She tried to hide her worry but when David was ready to go to the shuttle bay she started to cry. Please take care of your self honey. I will Heather you'll see it will all turn out just fine David replied in his new voice. I have to do this Heather for the sake of all of the people that died.

Then Heather said I don't know maybe its just that new voice of yours that gives me the willies. I know what you mean honey but it doesn't hurt me and its kind of cool. I never had a voice like this before and David started laughing to try to calm Heather down. Then Heather smiled and said, Ok honey I will have faith that you know what you are doing. But I know you and your just trying to make it look like that so I wont worry. Then David was ready to go and Heather wanted to go to the shuttle bay with David. So they headed down to the shuttle bay number 10. The shuttle Captain was all ready and waiting for David and Captain Dopar was going to go with David for back up. David felt very secure with that because Captain Dopar was a good man and David was starting to get use to Captain Dopars appearance. David looked at Captain Dopar and said, I couldn't ask for a better man.

Thank you for backing me up Captain its an honor to have you with me. Captain Dopar told David, no thank you. This is a very brave thing that you are doing sir. David said thank you but you would do the same thing. David gave Heather one last kiss. David just looked into her eyes and said you know I love right? Then Heather said yes I do and you know I love you more than anything in the world so you better come back sweetheart. David said Don't worry honey I will I promise!

GODS CHOSEN ONE

Chapter 12

T HEN DAVID AND the Captain loaded up onto the shuttle eagle. Their Pilot was Captain Briggs and his copilot Ensign Rice plus one assistant for loading and unloading. Finally you could hear Captain Briggs say shuttle Eagle we are ready for departure. Then we heard copy that, shuttle Eagle you are clear for departure. Then the shuttle pulled away and off they went to the surface in a pretty straight descent for one more final time hopefully. As they approached the surface structure they had about 15 minutes before the plasma field would engage. David readied himself emotionally and said to Captain Dopar what ever you do Captain do not risk getting hurt to save me. Just wait for the field to disengage if I need help, ok. Captain Dopar agreed with David, then the Commander went over to the air tight loading room and opened the door and he put his helmet on, gave Captain Dopar a wink and turned on his suit and got inside of the shuttle door and it sealed good and tight. Then David opened the outside door and got out and went to the structure. They were about ten yards away from it and David started to walk towards the base of the structure. Everyone was watching onboard the new Aurora and everyone on the shuttle Eagle. But the only people that knew about what they were doing was just a hand full of people. There was only two minutes left before the plasma field was to engage.

David was starting to talk to himself. I can't believe I am doing this. Well God I am putting my faith totally in you and I pray for a good outcome. I hope this time machine still works. Oh boy there's only 20 seconds left. I hope this works, David gritted his teeth. Then David said 5, 4, 3, 2, 1. Then suddenly the field came on and David was still standing in front of the field. Then he just started to walk into the plasma field. Then he disappeared into the field. On the Aurora, Heather was watching when David started to walk into the field, Heather said what are you doing honey don't walk into the beam.

There was still 3 full minutes before the field would stop. Everyone was starting to worry. Then finally the beam stopped and David was just still standing in the middle of the structure base. He appeared to be ok. Then Heather smiled and shouted out he's ok.

I knew you could do it honey. Commander Craft had taken over David's station and suddenly a led display light started to flash on David's console. Commander Craft spoke out and said Admiral we are experiencing some sort of a weird phenomenon. I can't tell if we are starting to orbit Venus or wait a minute sir the planet Venus is starting to rotate at a slow speed and its increasing in speed sir. Suddenly everyone looked at the view screen. The planet Venus started to rotate faster than it did. What the hell is going on replied Admiral Benson.

Commander Craft spoke out again and said sir the planet Venus is now going four times its normal rotation speed and sir it is not slowing down. Everyone was watching. The planet Venus was starting to spin faster and faster like a top. Admiral, Venus is now going 40 times its normal speed and is still climbing sir, Commander Craft said what the hell next is going to happen now. Everyone started to get a frightened look on their faces. Then Commander Craft said, Admiral we are starting to get pulled into its orbit. Suddenly the Aurora was starting to move. I suggest we counter with our impulse engines sir.

Very good Commander, Lieutenant, counter the pull of Venus's orbit. Yes sir Lieutenant answered. Admiral we have a problem our engines are not stopping us from spinning. Admiral for some strange reason we can't pull away from the draw of the planet. Also we can't go into light speed like this sir, if we did we would hit the planet Venus at this angle. We are just going to have to ride it out Lieutenant, the Admiral replied. Go to red alert Lieutenant. Yes sir, then we started going faster and faster. Then you could see all of the alert lights blinking on and off with the navy whistle going. Everyone was hustling to their stations to get buckled in. Everyone was strapped in when all of the sudden you could see the stars encircling everywhere and all of the lights had trails behind them. Then it was a bright light and then the Aurora vanished. Then everything started to slow, it seemed like the whole galaxy was spinning out of control on the view screen. Suddenly Venus started to slow down and then there was a huge explosion of light and suddenly the Aurora reappeared and inside you could see everybody reappear on the bridge. Then Venus stopped spinning and everyone woke up. Everything seemed normal. The ship was still on red alert and the Admiral said is everyone ok? Then the Admiral said does anyone know why we are on red alert? David was no longer on the planet Venus. He was at his station and Captain Dopar was not on the bridge at all. Then David spoke up and said it worked.

I'll be dammed, Then shouted, it worked! Admiral do you or anyone on the bridge know what just happened. Everybody shook there heads no, in confusion and said out loud, no sir. Then the Admiral replied I don't remember anything. Do you know what happened Commander. Then David got a big smile on his face and said yes sir I do, and started laughing some more. Sir your not going to believe this one, but here goes. Admiral and everyone else, we just went through one hell of a time warp. This is all happening to you because in our other time zone we were surprised attacked by the Arcons and the Thracians and so was earth and so was Sybon and Mars too. There were billions dead. We won, but it was real costly. Most of our ships were also surprised attacked and a lot of them were destroyed. The Arcons had developed new shields to where they were totally invisible. We couldn't see them coming. We were almost destroyed but we were able to get our shields to work and the Powleens also saved us at the very end. The Admiral was looking at David like he was crazy.

Sir to make a long story short, we found a time machine on the surface of Venus. I am the one that figured out how it worked. I sent us back in time before we were attacked so we could have everyone put on our Martian shields before we are attacked again. Admiral after checking the time zone now it appears to be a full day before we were attacked sir. Wow Commander when you say you know what happened.

You aren't kidding around are you sir? David answered no sir Admiral, what I am saying is the Gods honest truth. Man that's quite a story Commander. You know something Commander I believe you because I kind of feel it to. Then everyone else on the bridge looked at David and gave the look of acknowledgement that something did happen but they didn't quite know what it was. Lieutenant Courtney contact the President's office on Earth. Tell the President I will communiqué him in 20 minutes priority alpha. Yes sir Lieutenant Courtney replied. Then we have to contact Sybon and Mars and lets see if we can convince them of our story. We will have a full day to convince them all. Congratulations are in order Commander. Well done.

By the way Commander what time tomorrow should we be expecting our snake friends? David replied Admiral they will hit us right at 17.34 hours tomorrow in the afternoon sir. All of you are lucky you don't have to go through what I went through. If I could forget it I would. Then the Admiral said, Commander you are going to have to write a report on what happened in the other time zone for our logs some day. I know sir, David answered. Maybe I'll write a book too sir. Lets see where we were at on the genesis? Ah yes here we are. Wow this is weird trying to figure out where we are in this time zone now sir.

We are launching all of the canisters. We should have most of them on the surface by the end of today. Admiral after we warn everyone, I recommend we act like nothing is going on as far as the invasion is concerned. I agree with you Commander. Then David said, oh and sir this is very important! When everyone see's the flashes of light on the view screen and don't know what they are, please prepare yourselves because it is three Arcon battle cruisers and a Thracian star fighter fixing to hit us with a full attack with all new weapons sir.

Admiral I can't wait to surprise them snake bastards with our shields on. You have no idea what I have been going through for the last thirty days sir. Then the Admiral said, Commander I sure can't wait to read that report. Well theoretically speaking if we catch the Arcons and the Thracians by surprise what will we do with them. I mean, do we wipe them out or try to take them prisoners. I will have to ask the President about this one. I guess the right thing to do is to offer them a chance to survive in a prison. You know if they did this to us maybe we should go and invade their world and take it over and make their home planet their prison. That way we wouldn't have to keep them on any of our planets and its kind of poetic justice too. They were going to do that to us and they were going to eat some of us maybe our women and children. You know the more I look at this maybe we should blow them away. I think that's what I am going to recommend. They are to barbaric. Then David said sir, one more thing in the war in the other time zone we had a very effective way of combat with our ships. Once we had our shields on, what we were doing is firing on one enemy ship with the old weapons until about twenty or thirty of them were firing on one of our ships, then we would open fire on them all with the Martian weapons all at once. These Moon ships have over 1,000 weapons onboard. Only about 40 % of the weapons though have the capability of firing the Martian weapons. Which is quit adequate. They were popping like pop corn in the other time zone sir, and they couldn't do nothing. Well you'll see soon enough Admiral. Because sir, this time we will have the upper hand and guess what, we get to have all the fun too. I can't wait. I can't wait either Commander, the Admiral replied.

Commander Craft take over the bridge because I am going to my office to Communiqué the President and get a plan going on what we are going to do with these snake monsters. I have to tell you though. The thought of one of them sons of bitches eating one of our children or anyone is enough for me to recommend wiping them out. They are only going to be trouble anyway. To be honest with you I don't think you can trust a snake or teach a dog new tricks. David spoke up and said sir, lets not forget that they did kill over 15 billion people on Earth, Mars, and Sybon all combined in the other time zone. I never thought I would say this about any race or world. But I think the galaxy would be better off without these evil bastards sir. Then the Admiral spoke up and said I have to go talk to the President and got up and said the bridge is all yours Commander Craft and that he would be back in a little while and left to his office. David started thinking that it would be better to inform his science department about what was going on because after all they are the science department. I will go to my office, no that's right everyone is in the cargo bay setting up all of the canisters to launch them to the surface. Why don't I just head for the cargo bay and tell everyone there. I will just get everyone to take a break and that's when I will tell them. David told Commander Craft what he was going to do and headed for the cargo bay where everyone was. When David arrived everyone was working their butt's off. They were all ready for a break anyway. It was Captain Freedman and Captain Dopar and also Lieutenant Plant and just about everybody in the science department and maintenance too. They had all of the canisters hooked up to the probe's on the deck on the cargo bay. Ready to load with the chemical mixes and then launch to the surface of Venus. David walked over to Captain Freedman first and ask him if he didn't mind taking a break for an important meeting for about an hour.

Captain Freedman said sure Commander, what's up now? You are not going to believe this one Captain, but it's true. I am going to have to tell everybody all at once though, but it's big. Will you go and tell everyone to take a break for an important meeting? Captain Freedman said yes sir and walked over to everyone and started to tell them. Everybody started putting down their tools and started walking over to David. As everyone came over to David he told everyone to just sit on the floor of the cargo bay where ever they were and preceded to tell them what was going on. At first everyone thought it was some kind of a joke or test, but David finally convinced them that it was true. David even told them that everyone was suppose to act like everything was normal.

He also told them about what the flashes of light were and to watch for them. Then David said we are going to have to work just a little longer today because of the briefing, to make up the lost time so tomorrow we start out just like we did on that morning. It won't be easy but we can do it. It will get us right, on the time zone. They all looked at each other kind of funning but agreed and after David finished briefing them everyone walked over to the Red Star lounge for a couple of drinks and a snack and then they were going to start launching the rest of the canister's to the surface. In the other time zone at this point before they all called it a day in about four and a half hours. They had almost all of the canister's on the floor of the cargo bay launched. This is going to be so cool stopping the Arcons tomorrow. I am going to go bananas waiting for tomorrow to happen. Then David told everyone not to kill them selves and just do what you can to catch up. But he said we had just finished implementing the Venus genesis before they attacked us tomorrow, So I hope we can reach that point before we take care of business. He told everyone good luck and headed back to the bridge.

Mean while the Admiral was in his office having his communiqué with the President telling him what was going on.

The President also thought that the Admiral was pulling his leg but he did convince him finally. They were both so excited about tomorrow and the President gave orders that they could either shoot to destroy them once and for all or that they could target their shields and weapons and put a tractor beam on them for tow. But he didn't know where they were going to put them, but if it looks like they are going to be trouble, blow them away. The President was telling the Admiral that he was going to have to communiqué Sybon and Mars and brief all of them, and if they come up with something different the President would contact the Admiral and clue him in. He thanked him for everything and said to thank Commander Braymer for him and all of the people on Earth, Mars and Sybon. The Admiral then said, you are all our angels in the heavens that watch over all of us and we sure do thank you for it.

Then the President said he had to go tell everyone and said end communiqué. The Admiral went ahead and grabbed some lunch and then headed back to the bridge. David had already returned to the bridge and was checking to see if there was anyway to see the Arcons on his instrument control panel. But there was nothing, no indication at all, even when we know there out there. Then David started thinking. You know, I better find out where I came back in this time zone.

Lets see, ah yes I came back right before I ate lunch with Captain Dopar in my quarters. So when I went to the cargo bay and met Captain Dopar before lunch, I changed everything from there. I don't think I changed anything that much, just my lunch with Captain Dopar.

From there on, everything is about the same except that the fact that we have a surprise for the Arcons. We just have to set it all up today just right. Then David said thank you lord for helping us.

Suddenly the Admiral walked into the bridge and seen David and said, your just the man I want to see. You know Commander the President thought I was crazy at first but I finally got him to believe me. Everyone thought I was crazy in the cargo bay too sir David replied. But everything in the cargo bay is set up for tomorrow sir. Very good Commander the Admiral answered. You know Commander I want to thank you personally for tomorrow. This is going to be spectacular, and I am the one who gets to tell the Arcons to surrender, I love it. You're the son I never had. David smiled and thanked the Admiral and said Admiral for a couple of hours I am going to study the Arcons and try to learn how to detect them on our instruments better.

You know, to see if the flashes of light we were seeing is the only way to detect them. We will still have something to go by even if it is just the flashes of light. I may be able to find something else though. Then the Admiral said I will go ahead and leave you to your work Commander because with all of the excitement I forgot that I have to do something in my office. Sounds great sir. Admiral Benson said I'm going to go Commander, I will be back in a little while, the bridge is yours Commander Craft. Yes sir answered Commander Craft.

Commander Craft came over and sat down in the Admiral's chair. The Admiral left the bridge and David preceded to start to find the Arcons on his instruments. He tried everything for about three hours but yet the only way seems to be the flashes of light. I've tried infer red and I've tried metal, radiation, electrical interference, radio waves and I have tried motion and debris. The only way does seem to be a visual of the flashes of light. Man they do have some good shields.

Oh well, I guess I will go to my office too and see how well they are coming along on the surface canisters in the cargo bay. David told Commander Craft what he was doing and left the bridge for his office. When he finally arrived everyone was going at it. They were so busy no one seen David come in. David walked over to Captain Dopar and Captain Freedman to talk to them and to see how everyone was doing. Captain Freedman was the first to see him and David said how's it going Captain? Real good Commander, Captain Freedman replied.

We are ahead of schedule Commander as you see we only have about 20 more to go. That may seem like a lot but it's not, we are organized now and moving about 5 probe's every half hour. I figure we have about two hours left and we will be done on the canisters but then we have to launch 78 Satellite applicators. That will take all day tomorrow sir. Very good Captain. All of you have done a great job down here. If it wasn't for all of you we would never get nothing done.

MAYBE YOU CAN FIGHT DESTINY

Chapter 13

I JUST WANTED you and everyone else that was part of this operation down here in the launching aspects to know, we will get a special patch to go on your uniform with a possible promotion to go with it. I can't thank all of you enough. I also wanted to tell you what was going on as far as schedule. It is up to you what you want to do but you can either work until you guy's get tired or you can work way over your normal time so we will be ahead of the game tomorrow when the Arcons attack. I really do not care which way you all choose because the genesis is not connected to the invasion tomorrow. I would like to implement the genesis before we get hit by the Arcons though. But I thought you might want to be done with everything so you all can watch all of the fun tomorrow. Then Captain Dopar walked over to say hi. How's everything going Commander, Captain Dopar asked? We are doing better than I thought Captain, David answered. How's it going Captain. I was just telling Captain Freedman what was going on as far as schedule goes on the invasion tomorrow. We have alerted

Sybon and Mars and I have a feeling that it's going to be quite a show. I can't wait to put them bastards in there place. Captain Freedman if all of you choose to finish at around 17:00 to day maybe everybody can work double time tomorrow morning so everybody can be free about an hour before they attack. So you can watch it in your quarters on your T.V. monitors. Well, all of you keep up the good work and I am going to my office to prepare everything for 17:34 tomorrow and then back to the bridge. The two Captains said see you later Commander and off David went to his office for about an hour and then he would be off to the bridge and then home. David finally finished at his office and then hurried to the bridge. When David arrived back at the bridge he went right to his station. I am going to try once again to see if I can spot the Arcons some how. But he could not see or find any indication of them coming. Then he realized just how good their shields were. No wonder we got caught with are pants down.

They are virtually invisible. David worked at his station for another 2 hours. Then he told Commander Craft that he was going to call it a day and go to his quarters.

Commander Craft agreed and granted him permission to leave the bridge. In the last time zone David did not help until a couple of hours before the attack. This time he would start helping in the morning hour's to get a jump on things. Mean while lets not forget on the out skirts of our solar system, Earths and Mar's routine was about to change for the better. Our arch enemy the Arcons and their friends the Thracians were rushing to catch Sybon, Mars and Earth by total surprise. They had no idea we were waiting for them. They were coming in a vast horde of war ships for our destruction and to enslave and colonize Earth, Mars and Sybon. They had plans to take over our solar system. So they thought! Lets not forget that there was an excess of 1000 ships. Also the Powleens had a fleet strength of over two thousand ships but about half of them were all over the place in the galaxy in the other time zone. But there not going to be now in this time zone. The Arcons were going all out to take over the entire universe.

They were not going to get away with it this time. This is sure going to be something to remember. Back at the bridge David gave up on trying to find a way to detect the Arcons and headed for his place. He didn't know if Heather would be there or not. Back on Menok's bridge, Menok was going over the invasion with all of his Men. (Menok) Dabol Check with all of the Kima group. I don't want anyone to ruin the attack. If anyone messes up this chance for glory, I will wipe out their family name on our planet Bejeon. I do not want anyone to fire until I give my command.

(Dabol) Yes Menok it will be done by your rule. We will annihilate all their men and enslave their women and eat their children. Then Menok looked intent at Dabol and said I even bet they are tasty too. Then they started laughing and watching the view screen of them coming up to the outskirts of Pluto. Menok got on his communicator and said to all of his invading force. Listen up this is Menok, I want everyone to wait for my word to fire. I want everyone to check in when you are in your positions. I want Demins fleet to totally surround Earth and target them big guns first I will take the smaller fleet to surround Mars. I want all other ships looking for all of their ships. As soon as possible I want them in position because we will have to wait on you.

Now lets do it now. Then all of his fleet started to split up, all of them totally invisible. All of them had a kind of feeding frenzy look on their faces. They were a very carnivore race of people. But they had no idea what was before them. The Admiral was in his office planning the attack with Earth and Sybon and also Mars. The President was saying, that if you do not have shields that will project, and you can not stop the Arcons from leaving your area, the President gave permission to destroy the enemy. The President also said after all they would have done a lot of damage if Commander Braymer hadn't fixed everything.

Under no circumstance do I want you to risk all of your lives or any of your lives for that matter. But if they do not cooperate I would rather you destroy them, than them get away so they can do more damage at another time. I want to finish this once and for all. They shouldn't have came back. Also look what they were going to do to us. In fact they did it to us in another time. I am glad I am in this time zone because of them doing that to us. Can you imagine them eating us or our woman and children. They are nothing short of monsters. They deserve their fate! The more I think about it the more I want to destroy them. I am telling you this Admiral just so you know my frame of mind. The Admiral spoke up and said I am glad you told me this Mr. President because I fill exactly the same way as you. We may not ever get this kind of chance again Mr. President. I am for wiping out as many as we can. But Mr. President I am speaking now from an Admiral's stand point but I would like to have all of their ships we can get our hands on sir. I wouldn't mind having their cloaking device too. All we would need is a couple of their ships but we could make our fleet even bigger the more ships we get. You are right sir they deserve their fate.

I agree Admiral, I will give the orders to try to salvage as many of their ships as we can. You know Admiral when we project our shields on their ships they will have no choice but to surrender or we will blow them out of the heavens. So I know we will get some of their ships that way. Also Admiral I wanted to tell you the Powleens have to wait until the Arcons start the attack but when they do, The Powleens are going to invade the Arcons and the Thracians home planets. I was thinking, we could keep them in prison on their planet so we do not have to have them on our planets. Then the Admiral said I like this plan sir. Mr. President our ship the Aurora does not have the projection shields yet. We do have the regular Martian shields and the Martian weapons. We just haven't had the upgrade yet to the projection shields.

And we have no knowledge of where their shields are on their ships so we could target them. Or we do not know where to target their weapons either on there ships. In case we wanted to take them prisoner. So we really have no choice but to terminate them sir. We can give them one chance to surrender after we engage our shields but if they don't, well sir, I think you know what we have to do. Well then you know what you have to do then Admiral the President said. Yes sir I do the Admiral replied. Well sir, I hate to leave good company but I have to get ready on this end sir. Thank you for everything Mr. President. No Admiral Thank you and don't forget to thank Commander Braymer from all of us on Earth too. We owe you all our life's. One more quick thing. After we win the war with the Arcons we are going to throw a party on all three planets Admiral. I am going to suggest we make it a holiday. So tell everyone to plan on it. I have to go Admiral so tell everyone to take care. Thank you sir and Admiral Benson said computer end communiqué. Back at David's quarters he was just arriving home from work and Heather wasn't there but he had a feeling that she was coming by in a while as soon as she thought David would be home. David went ahead and took a shower for when Heather did come over today. David was kind of hoping Heather would stay the night. After David's shower he got dressed and then he gave Heather a call to see if she was coming over tonight to watch a sci-fi space adventure.

Or a pirate movie or something else. They have been watching a lot of comedy's lately and they were wanting to watch an old sci-fi space adventure called Moon People. It was a big hit in 2010.Television movies and video games were a big topic and was just about everyone's hobby in space when they were alone at home.

Everyone always got together at holiday's and played a lot of different type of card games. They had some local video game rooms for all the kids. They also had some sports like basket ball and bowling, pool and of course we had the largest assortment of video games that everyone competed against, adult and children. We even set up a big walk in theater for everyone to get together to watch a new release from Earth. Heather called and said she was coming over after her and Lieutenant Parsons the copilot did some shopping at the mall close to Heather's place. So David decided to have a nice dinner waiting for Heather when she did come over. He was also hoping she would stay the night. In the other time zone David had asked Heather to marry him but he hadn't done it in this time zone yet. He was thinking when would be the best time to ask her to marry him. He wanted to wait for just the right time. He was thinking maybe he might ask her after they win the war with the Arcons. But he wasn't sure, wait a minute why don't I ask her after the war and maybe we can be the first humans to get married on Venus. She would like that. That's what I will do then.

David went all out on the meal he was preparing for Heather and ordered lobster and shrimp and also a steak and shrimp dinner for Heather. That was her favorite meal. It worked out perfect, right when Heather came over David had just finished setting up the dinner.

Heather was all decked out and she was looking pretty. When she seen the dinner David had set up, she gave David a big hug and a long kiss and they went ahead and ate and watched the movie Moon People and of coarse had a few drinks. They had a good evening and then went to bed. David could not get his mind off of tomorrow. That's all he was talking about. He had to take a sleep aid to get to sleep then he finally fell to sleep. It didn't seem to long before the alarm went off and it was going to be the day to remember. Heather and David got up and got dressed. David ordered breakfast for both of them and set it all up on the table for them and when heather came out of the shower she seen that David had already set up breakfast and said you know honey I can sure get use to this kind of treatment. I am so use to doing everything myself. I don't know how to act but I sure do like it.

Heather gave David a great big kiss and they sat down and ate a good breakfast. Heather knew that David couldn't wait to go to the bridge and to get ready for the invasion. So she gave David a sinuous kiss and Heather told David that maybe later on after work that they could have another dinner and afterwards make love.

Then David smiled and said I would really like that. It's just that I have been so busy lately. I promise to make up for it though. Then Heather said alright then I will hold you to that. Then David said ok honey and gave Heather another kiss and off they went each going in their own direction. As David arrived at the bridge, he was early as usual. Commander Tice was still there from the night shift.

RIGHTING THE WRONG

Chapter 14

HELLO COMMANDER BRAYMER, how's things going with you today. David replied with a funny smile on his face. I am doing really good Commander Tice. I think all of us will be in a good mood by this evening. Commander Tice started laughing and replied we owe it all to you commander. I have been meaning to ask you Commander who all died in the war in the other time zone.

David gave Commander Tice a wield look and said, do you really want to know this Commander? I don't know why, but yes I do Commander, Commander Tice answered. Then David said, Well sir, since you are my commanding officer I will tell you. Commander Tice you were killed in the first assault and our co-pilot Lieutenant Tawny Fisher was also critically wounded but survived but with all kinds of health problems and in a wheel chair, Also Ensign Baker also died on the bridge in the first strike. Many other people died in that time zone.

Admiral Benson had a compound fracture on his arm and had a broken leg also. I had a broken arm, a head injury and I hurt my leg but it did not break. Everyone on the bridge had some kind of injury.

Earth and Sybon and Mars had all together about 18 billion deaths and twice as many injury's, but we are changing that right now Commander. We are going to have a entirely different outcome this time. Commander Tice looked at David kind of eerie and said I owe you a lot more than everyone else does then. No you don't Commander. I am doing what anyone else would be doing, even you Commander. I do not want you to put more into this than that Commander.

Commander Tice smiled and said you know Commander it just seems that we owe everything to science and technology these days. But I do appreciate what you did for us and I will never forget it Commander. Well Commander your welcome David replied. Then Commander Tice said, anytime you need anything please do not hesitate to ask Commander. David looked at Commander Tice and smiled and said thank you Commander but I am just doing my job.

Then Commander Tice said anytime my friend. David walked over to his station and started checking out all of his instruments. Most of the time his station is on auto.

But some times Captain Dopar is helping David at his station, when David isn't there. But Captain Dopar the last couple of days has been helping in the cargo bay with the launchings of all of the probes and satellites. David was going to try and detect the Arcons one more time at his station while they might be getting close to us. David started to go hard at it when in walked Admiral Benson. Hello there Commander, your just the man I wanted to see. We received a Communiqué earlier this morning from Mars. It was Venal the ruler of Mars, He was telling us that his Martian scientist name Barco something or other, I couldn't pronounce it again if I tried, warned us not to use the microwave beam on the core because of the plasma field anomaly. He said that it took a lot of energy to generate that kind of power like our magnetic plasma field. And that it was to dangerous to hit it with the microwave beam. Yes sir David replied, I am familiar with the danger of the plasma field from the last time zone Admiral. Oh I forgot about that Commander. That's alright Admiral you didn't know. Sir what did the President say about what to do when we catch the Arcons off guard today? The President said and I concur that we have an option that we can make an offer for them to surrender but if they don't they should be terminated. Mainly because we do not have the capability to project our shields around the enemy ships, like some of our other ships that upgraded their shields. We do have the Martian shields and weapons though and that maybe enough to do the trick.

Well Commander thanks to you we are going to have some fun later on. Lets see it's 0700 and you say they do not attack until 1734 hours later on. That's approximately 10 hours from now. That's when I almost died, Wow. What are you going to do with your time Commander? Well sir David answered, I have been trying to see if I could spot the Arcons and the Thracians on our instruments sir, one more time while they are real close. Then I was going to go to the cargo bay sir to help with all of the launchings of the satellites. Then we can have a little break before we watch the show sir. Also I will tell you Admiral no wonder we didn't see them coming. Sir except for the flashes of light up close, there is no way that I can find so far to detect them. They are virtually invisible Admiral. The only time you can see the flashes of light is when they are right next to us and we are in a lot of danger. Your right Commander, I don't like that part either. That sounds like you have a busy day before you, said the Admiral. Sir David said, I also wanted you to know that Captain Dopar has helped a lot sir. I can't tell you how valuable that man is Admiral. It was a little hard at first to get use to their appearance but knowing what I know now, I wish we had a thousand more of them on board. Yes I know what you mean Commander, the Admiral replied. Admiral is there anyway that we can give him an commendation for everything that he has done for us. Can you make him a Commander sir. He's earned it.

Commander we have over fifty Powleens on board and everyone say's the same thing you just did. I've decided to give them all a raise in rank but their world has to give it to them or its no good on their world. But maybe we can make it active on our ship while there here with us. Well Admiral I was going to head on down to the cargo bay to help them get done quicker. Ok Commander I will see you in a little while after you are done. Are you coming back to the bridge to be apart of the show, after all, this has been your show all the way from the beginning? Yes I believe I will sir. David smiled and said thank you for the invite sir. The Admiral starting laughing and said, ok then we will see you on the bridge later on then. David said, ok sir and headed for the cargo bay. On the way to the cargo bay David ran into Captain Dopar. He was also on his way to the cargo bay too.

Hello Captain how's things going with you my friend, the Captain bent his long neck down to where he was head level with David's and smiled and said I am doing good. I wanted to thank you for what you are doing for my people. I knew from the start that it was right to join your people. You are the most courageous and adventurous people I've seen throughout the galaxy and I have been in space off and on for about sixteen of your years. It is an honor to know you sir. Thank you Captain but it has been the one thing in my life that I can say that was good and that was meeting you and your people Captain, David replied. I want you to know that I recommended you for a promotion. We know it won't count until your people do it but the Admiral and I thought that on this ship you could have a higher rank. You should know that we do not give rank that easy either. You have earned every bit of it. You're a great science officer and a good asset on the Aurora. I wouldn't want to be without you, David said. Thank you sir. Then the Captain straighten his head and neck back up. He was 7 ft. 9 inches because of his elongated legs and neck and arms. Their uniforms were their own. They were mostly white with some green and blue in the trim around the neck. One Powleen did the work of at least two people some times three. As they arrived at the cargo bay everyone was already at it.

David and the Captain walked over to Captain Freedman and Lieutenant plant they were programming the satellite applicators. You could see satellites lined up all over in the cargo bay. David spoke up and said I thought I would come down and help get all of the satellites up and launched. So we could all watch the invasion on our home monitors after we have our shower's. Everyone laughed and said we can't wait for the Grand Finale. So everybody reorganized and went hard at it. One after another just like clock work. One section would program the satellites and another section filled the photosynthesis chemical mixture and then the last section launched the satellites.

Every now and then some one had one that seemed to defy logic. We just had to keep rebooting it until it would take. Some times it took about 10 times of rebooting. They were getting way ahead of schedule. They only had about twenty more satellites left to program and launch and it was only 1100 hours. It would only take probably about two more hours before we were done. That would give me plenty of time to shower up and go to the bridge for the attack. This is working out great. I can't wait. They took about a 5 minute break and then they went at it to finish up all of the satellites. Finally it came down to the last two satellites and then they were done. They finishes a good two and a half hours before the last time zone did. Then everyone went to the Red Star lounge for a couple of drinks before they left.

They sat in the same booth as they did in the last time zone. They hadn't seen any flashes of light yet probably because they finished earlier than they did in the last time zone. Right as they were finishing there drinks Lieutenant Plant seen a flash of light. I just seen a flash, See there it is again. Everyone seen it and then David said ok I am going to the bridge to see if we can detect these bastard right next to us on my instruments on the bridge. Everyone thanked Commander Braymer for helping and everybody went their own way to go home so they could take a shower and watch the attack. David rushed to the bridge to tell the Admiral that he had seen the first flash of light. As he arrived the first thing the Admiral said was we just seen one of the flashes off of the planet Venus Commander. David said, Yes I know sir so did all of us in the cargo bay. That's why I hurried here to tell you sir. Admiral I would like to try once more to detect any type of sign of their presence's besides the flashes of light sir. Or maybe we can find something so we could be able to track them some how. Maybe we can have some type of warning next time sir.

Yes that's some good thinking Commander. I am glad your on our side. David smiled and said thank you sir. When can we initialize the genesis Commander? Actually Admiral from here on out we can do everything from the bridge. Would you like me to activate the Venus genesis Admiral. All I have to do is send the order from the bridge to the canisters on the surface and then do the same thing on the satellite applicators. (Admiral Benson) Lets go ahead and initialize the genesis Commander. Very good sir, David replied. Engaging the canisters on the surface for the release of the chemical mixture now sir. And finally I am engaging the satellite applicators now too Admiral. Admiral the Venus genesis is now in operative mode. It will take three day's for the process to finish. Then the Admiral said very good Commander. Lets hope for the best on that one Commander. Now all we have to do is get ready to be attacked. Lieutenant Courtney I want you to communiqué the armament department and tell them to have them shields ready to initiate on my orders. Yes sir, Lieutenant Courtney replied. Two minutes later Lieutenant Courtney said Admiral the Armament has acknowledge their readiness sir.

Captain Welch in charge of the armament department said that they just finished hooking up an auto return fire on our weapons and a auto on, on our shields after the first initial attack incase we do not turn on our shields in time for any reason sir. The Admiral said to Lieutenant Courtney. Tell Captain Welch well done from me Lieutenant. Yes sir Lieutenant Courtney answered. Well I feel much better knowing that about the shields. It was the first strike that killed and injured everyone though. So we better get those shields up on time. Lieutenant Courtney I want you to ask the armament one more question. Ask them if there is anyway the enemy can detect our shields engaged? Yes sir Lieutenant Courtney replied. About two minutes later Lieutenant Courtney said Admiral, Captain Welch said he is pretty sure they can detect when our shields are on but he wasn't sure. Then the Admiral said to tell Captain Welch to be ready on my mark to turn on them shields. I do not want to take one hit if we don't have to here. Then suddenly everyone was watching the view screen and there was another flash of light. The Admiral was looking right at the screen. Then everyone said out loud there's another flash of light.

The Admiral looked at the LED Clock on the wall. It was 16:45 hours. There was only 49 more minutes left before the attack. Commander is there anyway that the enemy could fire early before the last time zone did? Unknown sir.

They didn't fire on us in the last time zone until we launched a probe to check out the flashes of light. They might have thought that we discovered their presence and fired on them, so they opened fire on us. Sir I suggest that you have them put on our shields right before you send a probe like last time. That's a good idea Commander but what if they can see our faces some how and they figure that we are on to them and fire early. Sir that is a possibility. Then the Admiral said you know what, why don't I give permission for the armament to put on our shields themselves when they see us get fired on in case they fire early, that's what I will do then. Lieutenant one more communiqué to the armament. Yes sir, the Lieutenant replied. Then the Admiral said I want you to tell Captain Welch to watch their view screens over towards the north west side of Venus and the minute they see them fire any kind of weapon, tell them I give you permission by your own will to turn them shields on. Ok Lieutenant. Very good sir, the Lieutenant replied. About two minutes later the Lieutenant spoke up and said Admiral

Captain Welch acknowledged what you said and said that he would monitor the view screen himself sir. He also said that if he sees them launch anything, them shields will be on sir. Very good Lieutenant. That makes me feel a lot better knowing that. Then David said yes me too sir. Well Commander we are coming down to the wire on this. I am sure glad we know the future on this one. I am sorry you went through all of this in a bad way in the last time zone. But I am sure glad you did what you did Commander. Then they all seen another flash of light. The Admiral grinned and said there it is again. David looked at the wall clock and there was still 20 minutes to go. Then it was down to ten minutes. I guess they didn't find out that we knew about the attack yet because they were still none responsive David said. Then the Admiral said you know what, why don't I communiqué Captain Welch on my uniform. Then the Admiral pushed the button on his coat and told the computer to contact Captain Welch. Captain Welch came on the call and said what can I do for you Admiral? Well Captain we have just a few minutes left and I was wanting you to turn on the shields right before we launch a probe in about 2 minutes Captain. The Captain answered and said I will do that sir on your mark. I will tell you by using my telecom on my uniform Captain. There was another flash of light and the Admiral said ok is everyone ready? Here goes. Then the Admiral said ok Captain Welch turn on them shields and launch that probe. Then Captain Welch said here goes.

You could see the Aurora launch the probe at Venus and just like in the last time zone you could see them fire a red light pulse toward the Aurora but this time the shields were on. It did nothing and that's when David smiled and realized that they pulled it off and changed everything for the better. There were three Arcon Battle Cruiser's and one Thracian Destroyer decloaking and then they opened up with everything they had. The Arcons just kept firing all of their weapons and it was useless. The Arcons were totally stunned that they were doing nothing. The Arcons were reporting back to Menok's ship.

Menok the Earthlings discovered us some how and they fired on us first or we wouldn't had fired back. You fools Menok replied that was just a probe. I talked to everyone about this in great detail before we left Bejeon. Their leader Menok was really angry at them because they fired on the Earthlings before he gave the order and gave away the entire invasion so he thought. He didn't know about David going back in time. He said he would blow them away himself if he was there. He told them that they better fight to the death and be victorious in battle or he was going to destroy their families name's by killing his whole family. The Admiral just let them fire for a while before he told Lieutenant Fisher to ready the Martian weapons and target all four ships at the same time. The Martian weapon has locked in on all four target's sir, Lieutenant Fisher answered. The Admiral told Lieutenant Courtney to tell our friends that they have one minute to stop firing their weapons and to surrender or we will open fire and destroy them.

Affirmative Admiral, the Lieutenant replied. Two minutes later the Arcons still refused to stop firing their weapons. The Admiral gave Lieutenant Fisher the order to fire. Lieutenant Fisher opened fire on all four ships and they all exploded like pop corn popping Boom, Boom, Boom Boom. The force did not hurt the Aurora because of the shields but it did throw them back and forth for about a mile in space from the Arcon ship's exploding. Admiral the Arcon ships have been destroyed.

The problem was eliminated sir, said David grinning from ear to ear. Then everyone yielded "Hurrah" for Commander Braymer. Everyone was waiting that day for the Arcons to attack. Everyone was laughing and talking, it sure was totally different from the last time zone. The Admiral said keep them beautiful shields on for a while Commander Braymer. Back on Earth, they were able to have their shields up and running and so did Sybon and so was Mars. All they were able to do was destroy almost all of our satellites.

The Admiral said lets high tail it to Earth and have some fun saving Earth and suddenly the Aurora left the Venus orbit on impulse and then you could see a flash of light and off they went to help save Earth.

CLEANING HOUSE

Chapter 15

THEY WERE ATTACKED on the way several times. Admiral Benson would just come out of light speed and sit there like we were hurt and wait for as many ships as he could get to fire on the Aurora. Then he would give them a chance to surrender and if they didn't he order their destruction. Then off towards Earth he would go again until someone else would fire on them. The Arcons were sure brave or maybe that Menok their leader was the meanest son of a bitch alive because none of them would surrender. We never did find out if Menok died or what. There were a lot of Powleen ships all around Earth and Mars too. They were blowing away all of the Arcon ships one after another. The Arcons thought that the more of their ships that fired on the one ship, the more it would weaken the shields and destroy our ships, but it was bringing them to their fate. We would just wait for as many ships as we could get to fire on us and then we would open up with the Martian weapons on all of them at once.

They didn't have a prayer because of the Martian shields. Venal the leader of Mars was running the show on Mars and worked with both the Powleens and Earth and everyone was saved. The Martians had all of their aircraft from before. They had over 800 fighter ships.

They were the size of one of our cars. But they had the Martian shield's and weapons on all of there ships already. The Martians were incredible. Their engines worked totally different from ours. It was like they had light speed capability for very short distances. They were unbelievable to watch they were so fast that they appeared and disappear for very short distances and then reappear again firing their weapons without the bang of a sound barrier or without a flash of light for light speed. They may have been small but they were as deadly as any of our Moon ships to the Arcons, but they could only fire four weapons at once. Buts that's all they needed. The Martians were waiting for as many of the Arcons to attack their ships, just like we did.

We had zero casualties in the war and so did Mars. The Arcons lost their entire fleet. Most of what didn't get destroyed was taken captive by our side. There may have been a select few that got away because of their shields but most of them were destroyed.

The Powleens went to the Arcons planet called Bejeon and the Thracians home planet called Maldin and destroyed 90 % of both worlds. The Powleens just pounded both planets with the Martian weapons. Then they would each drop off about 30 thousand troops on the surface where ever they were. It did not take long to take over both planets. They were defenseless against the Martian weapons and shields. Both Bejeon and Maldin fired everything they could possibly fire at the Powleens but to no avail. Nothing the Arcons had or the Thracians did could stop the Powleens. The Powleens did get some casualties on the ground take over but very few. The Arcons still had possession of a few of the out of the way places. But the Powleens had total domination of both worlds. They would be able to totally colonize both worlds soon. The Arcons and the Thracian worlds were not bad looking. The only thing that ruined it was them. But that soon was not going to be a problem. When the Powleens found a large group of Arcons or Thracians hiding they would project the Martian shields all around their area and imprison them with their shields. The Arcons would need a miracle to come back from this spot. That day the entire universe was reborn. Everyone loved David for what he did. He had card blanch at what ever planet he went to. He was the most famous person in the entire universe. Everyone rounded up all of the Arcons and the Thracians and said they were going to take them home and took them to their own home planets. What they didn't know until their long journey home is that the Powleens had already took their planets captive. Also that they were going home to be put in prison. All six planets made a holiday in remembrance for the victory of the war.

Everybody celebrated for a couple of weeks. We had a new universe and it was now in harmony. Mean while back on the Aurora Admiral Benson and the rest of the crew of the Aurora was living it up on Earth and in Earth's orbit. David was with Heather and they were at a popular vacation sight on earth on the beautiful Island of Jamaica.

David and Heather were on the beach swimming and playing around. At present they were in the surf splashing each other. David grabbed Heather and she splashed him in the face and ran from David on the beach and he couldn't see because of the salt in his eye's so Heather turned back to help David and he tricked her and grabbed her and they both went for a dunk. They came back up and they were both laughing and Heather gave David a very long kiss. David returned the favor and said you know there was something I was wanting to talk to you about. Heather smiled and said what do you want now and started giggling. David looked at her in her eye's and said how would you like being married to me. I mean have you ever thought of what it would be like married to me. Then Heather said wow. I had no idea we were going to talk about marriage. Then Heather smiled and said you know David I have thought about it and I just always figured that if I ever got married it would probably be with you. Then Heather asked why, are you going to propose to me now. Then David smiled and went over to his blanket and belongings on the sand and pulled out a little black box and opened it to show Heather. Then David said yes I was going to ask you to marry me today and if you said yes you could put this ring on.

Then David pulled out the ring he got for Heather and opened the box. Heather grabbed the box and said oh isn't that beautiful. It was a 3 caret pink flaw-less diamond. Then David said I thought that we could maybe be the first couple to be married on the planet Venus after the genesis. Then Heather looked at David with a very sexy look and said you know I would really love that and gave David another long kiss. David was so happy that he started to tickle Heather and he chased her all over the beach and they were having fun until it started to rain. Heather and David grabbed their stuff and headed back to the hotel with David chasing Heather. They made love when they came back to the hotel and had a great lunch and suddenly the phone rang. It was Admiral Benson and he was wondering if David wanted to go back to Venus to finish the Venus genesis project. David replied yes sir.

David and especially Heather wanted to go back to Venus to finish the genesis so her and David could get married. The Admiral said we have to report to NASA by Sunday morning for launch preparations for the shuttle launch back to the Aurora. It was Friday so they went ahead and celebrated a lot more and went dancing and went out to eat at another one of Jamaica's restaurants. Then they headed back to Miami. Time flew because it wasn't long before David and Heather were at launch preparations to go back to the Aurora. Dr. Blue was the ongoing Doctor with this shift. Heather and David were both hooked up to about twenty electrodes and did about 30 test. Before you knew it they were done. Then off they went to the shuttle Moon Beam, it was one of the shuttles that went to the Aurora. They were both strapped in and getting ready to launch. Before they knew it they were counting down to the launch. Captain Briggs was our shuttle Commanding Officer. He was certainly in a good mood.

He was joking with everyone. He ask David if he had went to the restroom before launch and said most people forget and then when we launch. David started laughing and said I went to the restroom but I do not know if Heather did. They both looked at Heather with a smile on their faces. Heather said we were suppose to go to the restroom before the launch. No one told me that. Then David said he's only kidding honey. Then the Captain started laughing again and said don't mind me, I am just fooling around. He said ok is everyone strapped in because if your not it might be a hard lift off for you and he grinned. Then it got down to 2:00 minutes and counting and before you knew it you could hear Captain Briggs say. NASA this is shuttle Moon Beam and we are go for launch. Copy that shuttle Moon Beam, you are go for launch sequence 2:00 minutes and counting. Copy that NASA. David looked over at Heather and she was gripping the arm of her chair with a steel grip. David was scared to but he didn't want Heather to see it so he put on one hell of a front.

Then it was lift off. 10, 9, 8, 7, 6, 5, 4, 3, 2, 1, ignition full thrust. That's when David gripped his chair. So did Heather and as the shuttle started sounding like thunder and a lot of vibration. Captain Briggs said NASA "We have lift off".

All systems are go. Then we started moving upward it was another perfect launch. Copy that Moon Beam your on your way now.

Your go down here. Your coarse is laid in and all systems look good. Roger that NASA, this is shuttle Moon Beam, see you on the flip side over and out. David and Heather were looking out into space with an awe look of amazement. The G force was right around 4 G's until they left the Earth's atmosphere. Then David and Heather started to relax a little bit and after that it was smooth sailing. As they were headed toward the Aurora David and Heather seen again how huge the Aurora really was, it took your breath away, no matter how many times you seen it. There were all kinds of Moon ships and all other kind of space ships in orbit around Earth. Everything seemed like it was a movie. As they were coming closer to the Aurora. You could see how vast space really looked and how beautiful it really was. Then we heard the shuttle Moon Beam and the Aurora. This is the USS Aurora do you read me? Roger that USS Aurora this is Captain Briggs on the shuttle Moon Beam requesting permission to come board for docking sir.

Shuttle Moon Beam permission granted, we need you to dock at number 10 docking bay over. Roger that USS Aurora, locking in computer data now sir. Docking bay laid in and we are now on Auto pilot. Copy that shuttle Moon Beam we will do the rest from here. The USS Aurora over and out. Docking went as smooth as butter. They made it look so easy. The lighting in space was phenomenal. We had to wait about 30 minutes before we could unload. They were glad to be home again. They all went to their quarters and took another shower and got dressed and David and Heather stayed together for a couple of hours and then David went to the bridge. When David arrived at the bridge everyone said their hello's. David was glad to be back. Now he could focus on the finale of the genesis project. The Aurora pulled away on impulse and then you could see a flash of light and off they went back to Mars. It only took about 25 minutes to get back. Then the Aurora slowed on impulse and then stopped off the planet Venus. The Admiral had to go to his quarters for about an hour. He was trying to find a certain document that he was looking for. He finally found it and put it in a safe location and then headed back to the bridge. David was ready to adjust the satellite ecliptic tint shields. Everyone was on the bridge that was normally on the bridge except for the Admiral. Then in walked the Admiral. The first thing he seen was David at his station and he smiled a big smile and said. There's the man of the hour.

Did you have a good vacation on Earth Commander? Glad to have you back Commander. Then David said, glad to be back sir.

Heather and I had a great Vacation. Also Heather and I got engage to be married in Jamaica. The Admiral put a big smile on his face and said well congratulation Commander. I was wondering when you two were going to get hitched. Admiral, David replied we were also going to be the first couple to get married on Venus if the genesis works out with your permission sir. We were also hoping that you might marry us on Venus. Wow I am honored Commander. It would be my pleasure. I just hope the genesis turns out to where we can Commander. Once again congratulation Commander. Then David started talking to the Admiral. You could hear David asking the Admiral if he was ready to adjust the eclipse satellites to let a certain amount of sun through to finish the Venus genesis project. The Admiral replied, You know it sure took a long time to get to this one point didn't it Commander. David looked at the Admiral with a funny look and said you sure do have that right Admiral. Are you ready to finish this genesis project sir? Affirmative Commander. Lets finish this project.

The Admiral walked over to his chair and got prepared for the finish. Everyone was watching on all five planets, on their T.V. monitors. Ok here goes said David, I have been wanting to do this for a long time. Adjusting the shields now sir then you could see the planet Venus start to come out of the eclipse. David adjusted the amount of Sun very slowly for the temperature to rise to about 80 degrees Fahrenheit gradually and was constantly readjusting the tint and then you could start to see the snow melt. Then you could see a storm front starting to form at a lot of locations on the surface. Then it started to rain. The planet Venus was coming to life. It was looking like Earth.

The genesis was working. Something no one expected was, is that the planet started changing colors right in front of them. Because of Venus being eclipsed for so long the genesis was looking very successful. There wasn't a lot of water but there was a few rivers going.

Admiral the satellite tint is set sir. We will probably have to adjust it several more times before we get it right. Admiral there is a lot of different toxic chemicals in the atmosphere. We were expecting this but now we have Oxygen and Admiral the Carbon Dioxide levels is now down to 23 % and still falling very slowly. Nitrogen is up to 70% sir and the surface pressure is 12.7 psi, that's close to Earths pressure and it's stable too sir.

I was wondering about this aspect but it appears that it worked out perfect. I believe it worked so well because of the fact of on Earth we have almost 20 billion people that is constantly breathing in Oxygen and breathing out Carbon Dioxide. On Venus there is no life yet, so once we get rid of the Carbon Dioxide its gone for good. We have filtering systems that the Powleens have developed that we can place in certain locations to filter out the toxins, Admiral. We need to use about twenty or thirty of them atmosphere thermo hydro filtering systems on the planets surface. We ordered them and they should be here sometime today. That will be are next project. We can now walk on Venus but we will still have to wear suits until we filter most of the toxins out of the air. That would take about thirty of Venus's days. Then everyone was saying it's looking like Earth. Venus was looking good. Everyone started shouting hurray for Commander Braymer.

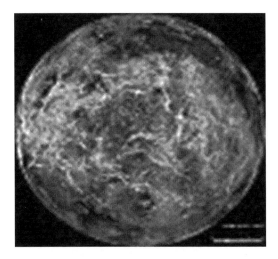

Then David said hey everybody all of you did this not just me. So I say hurray back to you. We have come a long way because now we can have a Venus base at this point on the surface. Soon we will be able to rid the toxins and then we can colonize it. We will still have to wear our suits though until we get the air clean. But that won't take very long only about 30 to 60 solar Venus days. David stayed at it at his station for a couple more hours and then he was going to take lunch. Admiral we've done about as mush as we can do.

Now all we have to do is let the photosynthesis finish its work. Admiral request permission to go for lunch sir. Permission granted Commander, and Commander great job. David said thank you sir and got up from his station and headed to his quarters for lunch. When David finally arrived at his place, Heather was waiting for him with lunch. Heather gave David a kiss at the door and then they went to the dinner table to eat. Heather set up a pot roast with all of the trimmings.

David said wow honey this is a nice lunch. I bet I get so full I wont want to go back to work. Did the genesis work to where we can get married David, Heather asked? David smiled and said well honey I have some good news and some bad news. Oh no, you mean we can get married now, what's the bad news? Heather asked? David said honey, we can still get married but we have to do it with our air suits on.

Unless you can wait up about 30 to 60 days. Then we will probably be able to get married without air suits. That's about how long it would take for the big thermo hydro filtering systems the Powleens made to work. They made the hydro filters to filter the air enough to live on Venus without air suits. We put some of these on Earth too.

David spoke up and said it could take longer than that honey, there's no way to know until we start the filtering systems. That's a tough question maybe we should wait Heather replied. Honey we have already ordered the thermo hydro filtering systems and they are on there way they should be here either later on today or tomorrow morning. The Powleens will set them on the surface and get them going, after that all we have to do is wait. It might not even take as little as thirty days honey. We wont know until we get them going. Then David said I will leave it up to you if you want to get married in our air suits or wait.

Then Heather relaxed a little bit and gave David a kiss and said your right sweetheart. I will wait and see and I promise to be more patient. Your doing fine David replied, don't worry we will get married as soon as possible. I tell you Heather how many people can say they were the first ones to be married on the planet Venus. Your right David I just hope it doesn't take forever to get the air clean on Venus. It won't you'll see honey. Then they kissed again and they ate so much David didn't want to go back to work. I am so stuffed. I wish I could stay with you honey but then David said he had to go back to the bridge and get back to work. They gave each other a final kiss and off he went back to the bridge.

When he arrived back at the bridge he checked to see how far away the Powleens were and they were almost already there. So they would be here today that's great David said. Soon after that the Powleens started to arrive and place the Thermal Hydro Filters on the surface of Venus and activating them. Venus was looking so beautiful now. The Powleens were so impressed with us Earthlings from how good our genesis's on Mars and Venus was coming out. It wasn't long before they had all of the filtering systems in place on the surface up and running. A few Venus days went by and the filters that the Powleens made were working exceptionally well because there was no people on the planet yet. It was not going to be as long as David thought. A couple more weeks went by and the atmosphere was looking good. There was plenty of Oxygen on the surface. There was still some Sulfur and a few other things in the atmosphere but the filtering systems were paying off. The poisons in the atmosphere were starting to diminish you could probably take the atmosphere for about three days before you would have to be put on Oxygen. There have been several expeditions on Venus checking out not only the huge filters but all of the terrain and searching for more alien artifacts like the Eye Of God" time machine. The Martians also had several missions on Venus for exploration. Venus was looking like a major success. David was starting to acknowledge that it was just about time to try and take off the air suits. He was going to give the order to take off the suits soon.

The air was showing minimal toxins in it and Venus was looking fantastic. It really hadn't hit everyone yet that it was almost time to colonize Venus. We would yet have another planet like Earth and Mars to colonize. Our solar system was getting bigger by the day.

The next shuttle mission with David was going to be the one to try to breath the air. David was going to be one of many to be the Ginny Pig's. He didn't mind because he new the air was clean pretty mush. In fact he was in a hurry so he could surprise Heather so they could get married. Then the Admiral gave the order and off everyone went to the surface of Venus for the final test. In the first shuttle was Commander Braymer, Captain Dopar, also Captain Freedman, and Barco from Mars even got in on the fun. The President thought it would be good diplomacy and last but not the least in their shuttle was Lieutenant Plant. There was three shuttles. The Admiral was in one and so was Commander Craft and Commander Tice. They were all going to be the first to go without air suits on Venus.

David wanted to do it that way so everyone in the science department and everywhere else could be involved more in the data statistics to be on record as the first to breath fresh air on Venus. They pulled over to a flat area and all three shuttles landed as easy as could be. There was so much color everywhere now. Green and brown all over the place. The green was from all of the photosynthesis mixture that had settled on the surface of Venus. It was like a moss type of growth. All of them had their suits on when they got out of their shuttles. David was going to go first while everyone watched for effect.

First they did some air testing and then David had Captain Dopar help take David's helmet off. David was holding his breath until he had his helmet totally off. Then the camera zoomed in on David's face. Then as everyone on all of the planets were watching David took his first deep breath and then gave a pleasant look and said it does smell a little funny but it smells good. It smells like there's a faint sulfur smell in the air but I can breath good. Everyone watched David for a second and then everybody agreed and David gave the ok and they took their air suits off. They were all waving into the camera and laughing. David first and then everyone else put their thumbs up for the camera. Then all of them totally took their entire suits off in front of the camera. Everyone was clapping for joy and smiling. Then David said wow just 2 and a half years ago it was only Earth that we knew about now we are connected to Mars, Sybon, and now Venus and Bejeon and Maldin. We now have five planets to colonize. David started laughing and said we really do have a federation of planets. Now Heather and I can get married on Venus. Boy is she going to be happy now. Heather was watching it all at David's home on the T.V. monitor. She immediately started planning the final details of the wedding. She was on cloud nine. The Admiral was going to be the one that married them.

Her brother Lieutenant Charles Courtney was going to give the bride away. Captain Dopar was going to be the best man. Lieutenant Gina Parsons the pilot was going to be the maid of honor and Lieutenant Tawny Fisher the Co-pilot was the brides maid. And of coarse there were going to be a lot of people from the Aurora and some of Admiral Bakers ship. There were a lot of Powleens going to attend the wedding also. There was even going to be some Martians there.

Venal and his wife was going to be there and a lot of other people too from Mars. It was also going to be televised on all of the 5 planets and all of the ships in the heavens that could pick up the signal.

It was going to be a spectacular event seen through out the galaxy. Heather was so happy. She planed the date to be two weeks from today. She didn't have to send out invitations because it was all being televised everywhere. She did have to tell her mother and make arrangements for her to come. Her father had past away when she was very young. Both of David's parents also had past away many years ago. David just felt they would be watching from heaven anyway.

Them two weeks flew by fast and before you knew it they were having the wedding on Venus. They had huge tents everywhere and chairs by the thousands and everyone else stood up. There were people everywhere too. It was a spectacular day. Finally you could here the wedding music and then you could see Lieutenant Charles Courtney was walking down the aisle with his sisters arm in his and as they approached the altar David was already standing there at the altar.

Heather was wearing a beautiful pure white wedding gown with a long wedding train and a long white veil. The train was so long it had two boys holding the end corners. As she reached the top of the altar the music stopped. David looked Heather in her eye's and said you look so beautiful. Thank you Heather replied you look great yourself.

David was decked out with a black tuxedo and looking good. Then Heather said well David are you ready for this. David looked intently into her eye's and said I wouldn't have it any other way. Then you could hear the Admiral start the vows. Today on the planet Venus where the Goddess of Love rules. We are having the first wedding ever on Venus. This historic wedding will unite this man and this woman in Holy Matrimony. Commander David Braymer do you take this woman to be your lawfully wedded wife to love honor and to obey for the rest of your life till death do you part? Then David looked at Heather and said I do! Lieutenant Heather Courtney Do you take this man to be your lawfully wedded husband to love honor and to obey for the rest of your life till death do you part? Then Heather looked at David with a glow in her eye's and said I do. Then the Admiral said do you have the ring Commander? David pulled out the ring and put it on Heather's finger then the Admiral said, by the power invested in me I now pronounce you Husband and wife. Then the Admiral said, you may kiss the bride.

Then David held Heather and they kissed a long kiss and then everyone in the crowd started cheering and throwing party streamers and rice. Then David and Heather were escorted to their shuttle that was all decorated where Captain Briggs was waiting.

Then off they went back to the Aurora where everyone set up a special honeymoon suite with flowers everywhere and a lot of champagne. Soon after that you could see everyone's ships pulling away form Venus and heading to their homes in the heavens. Nobody seen hide nor hair of David or Heather for about a week. Everyone in the heavens were in harmony. There was no more fighting or worrying about the Arcons. It was truly a great time to be alive in the universe.

Earth and Sybon and even some Martians started colonizing Venus and we still had to finish colonizing Mars. Now we could thin out the population of Earth and give everyone more room.

We had huge cargo ships full of trees and plants and plankton also animals, birds and a lot of building material. Construction was going on everywhere. But everyone stayed away from the "Eye of God". It was revered as a very Holy site. You could only view it from a distance. Everyone even colonized Bejeon and Maldin too. Mostly the Powleens though. We end this story by showing you a picture of the New Venus.

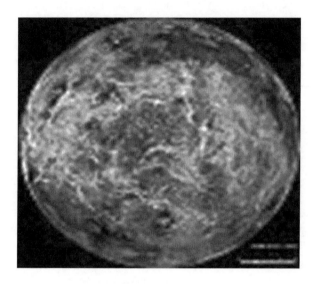

THE END

Made in the USA
Middletown, DE
11 March 2019